OPERA OBSESSED

OPERA OBSESSED

a novel

by

BRUCE K BECK

AUDACITY BOOKS
WE DARE TO TELL THE TRUTH

New York

This is a work of fiction. Names, characters, businesses, places, events, and incidents are either the products of the author's imagination or used in a fictitious manner.

This is a first edition from Audacity Books.
Please visit us on the web at www.audacitybooks.com.
For information about rights or purchases,
please email us at info@audacitybooks.com.

This book is dedicated to all the brave soldiers
who step onto opera stages and sing their
hearts out—and to those who love them.

Chapter One

Don't ask me why I took a chance. But if you've ever tried to navigate the intersection of Broadway, Columbus Avenue, and West 65th Street—right in front of Lincoln Center—then you know how confusing it is. And if you haven't tried to cross those streets, then please take my word that it's the most complicated roadway in New York City. It was just turning dark. The glare of headlights had started to play its games with perception. I looked both ways, and then I leapt into the street.

The next thing I knew there was a yellow cab bearing down on me. It stopped quickly, but not before it knocked me on my ass. I was stunned, of course. No one expects to be hit by a car. I tried to assess the damage, from my prone position. The driver got out of the cab, and then a young man dashed over from the pedestrian median that I had nearly reached, stood over me, and asked, "Are you okay?"

"Yes, I think so," I said.

"Do you need medical attention?"

"No, I don't think so, but could you help me up?" I asked.

"Of course," he said. And he did. Together we got me up and dusted me off. My new hero started snapping photos of the scene and the driver's ID. "Are you sure you're okay? Because you really should call for an ambulance right now if there's any chance of injury."

"No, I'm fine," I said. We walked to the median, releasing the cabbie from his awkward situation—stopped in the middle of a busy intersection. He sped off. "Julian Harcourt," I said, extending my hand.

"Stuart Kreisler," he said, as he shook my hand. I liked his hand. It felt strong and reassuring. "Give me your cell number, so I can text you these pictures," he said. I did, of course, and within seconds I had documentation of the accident scene plus Stuart's phone number. I reassessed my body, determining that it was indeed undamaged. I didn't tell Stuart that I was really more concerned about my clothing: Bodies will heal, but vintage Prada jackets? Not so much. That was also unscathed. Somehow. Stuart and I walked—carefully—across the remaining lanes of that thorny junction, to the plaza.

The splashing water in the fountain was refreshing, as always. I might almost have believed I had imagined the cab collision, except that I was walking with my new hero. "I'm going to the Met. Where are you headed?" I asked.

"I'm also going to hear *AÏDA* tonight. I'm a tenor, by the way, and my agent thinks she can get me work covering Radamès. If not here, then in other big houses."

"Aren't you in the wrong business?" I asked.

"Ha, ha, ha," Stuart said. No doubt he had heard that joke before—my reference to the great violinist whose surname Stuart shared. I could sympathize, since my own name says publishing through and through, and yet I'm an illustrator. "I'm sitting at a lectern with the score tonight, in the boxes, house-left," Stuart said.

"My friend Chris and I will be in our usual seats in the balcony. We love the acoustics there." And the price, I didn't mention. "I'll look for you at inter-mission," I said.

"I'd like that," he said. And then it was time for us to part and get on with our separate evening plans. I thanked him again for his kindness. And I promised to text him soon. Chris was waiting for me in the lobby, near the gift shop. I greeted her and gave her the capsule version of the last few minutes.

"Really, Jules, you have to be more careful. You seem to be taking chances all the time these days. I don't want to lose you," she said.

"Thank you, dear," I said. "But as you see, I'm perfectly fine." I was, of course. But there was other drama ahead—when we received our programs. Ac-tually, I hate *AÏDA*. I only agreed to it as part of our season because our new favorite soprano was sched-uled to sing the title role. Her first at the Met, I think. Chris was stoked, too. And then we arrived to dis-cover that she wasn't singing! Not because she was out sick—that happens, after all—but because she wasn't scheduled for that performance. We were dumbfounded—but resigned.

All through the first act I studied the lecterns to see if I could spot Stuart. That was much more en-tertaining than what was happening on stage. *Celeste Aïda* is nice enough. The rest of Act I? Not so much. I couldn't find Stuart, but no matter. Per-haps I'd see him at intermission, and if not, then I had his phone number for a follow-up thank you call. And a reunion? Who could say?

I did spot Stuart at intermission, ahead of me in line for the men's room. It's always a long line, but mercifully fast-moving (unlike the line for the ladies' room across the lobby.) He was finishing just as I was in range of the urinals. "Let me buy you a glass of champagne," I said as he passed me.

"Sure," Stuart said.

"I'll be right out." Chris was waiting for me in the middle of the lobby, in front of the champagne line. And Stuart happened to be waiting nearly next to her. That made introductions easy. The line moved quickly, just like the line for the men's room. I bought our drinks. We sipped them and made small talk. I didn't tell Stuart I hated the opera. I didn't think it fair to be so negative while he was learning a role. He did suggest that it was rather a lackluster production—for the Met. I still resisted the urge to badmouth anything. And so did Chris.

When we returned to our seats, I asked Chris, "So, what do you think of Stuart?"

"He seems very nice," she said.

"Yes, but that's not what I meant," I said. "I'm guessing he's straight. What do you think?"

"It's hard to say, with singers," Chris said.

I laughed and said, "Isn't that a bit general?"

"No, I'm serious," Chris said. "With all artists, just because they're not macho monsters, it's easy to jump to conclusions. Even when they're not real flamers."

"Which Stuart is not."

"Which Stuart is not," Chris agreed. "But really, Jules, are you sure you want to complicate your life with another singer? Are you looking for another long-distance romance?"

Ouch! I thought. The conductor entered the pit and started the Act II overture, so we fell silent. I managed to stay awake for most of Act II, but the intermission that followed it felt like a welcome relief. *Will I see Stuart again?* I wondered. I did, actually. And we shared another glass of bubbly. It was the best part of the evening, for certain. Two more acts, and the dreary old warhorse was finally put out of its misery—and we, out of ours. Chris and I were both shaking our heads in disbelief as we made our way out of the gilded palace, into the fresh air of the plaza, and into a taxi.

"Thank God the rest of our season has been glorious. And the last two should be, as well," Chris said.

"Exactly," I confirmed. The drive across the park on the 65th Street Transverse was quick and easy, as it usually is that time of night. And two minutes later we were in front of Chris's building. "Sleep well, darling," I said as she opened the cab door. "And don't forget dinner on Thursday."

"I'll be there," she said. "Jules, please be careful." I assured Chris that I would be careful. But assuring *myself* was a different matter. What did Chris mean when she said I'd been taking chances lately? Surely I'd been living my life, just as I always had. Surely there was no new element of risk. We waited until Chris's doorman welcomed her, and then the cabbie sped me to my building. It was a lovely evening, and yet I turned up my collar against a sudden burst of wind. And I got myself home. My solitary bed was waiting patiently for me.

I love that bed. It's a mahogany sleigh bed I found at an antique sale a decade ago. And the purchase included the original mattress, which is stuffed with horsehair and more comfortable than any other mattress I've slept on. And I've slept on a few, believe me. No, my bed is the real thing. And there have been moments when it's felt like the only constant in my life—my only haven. That night I brushed my teeth and put away all thoughts of phony ancient Egypt and duty and revenge and suffocation. I slipped into my bed and let it work its magic on me.

I was never a real opera queen. If I hadn't dated a singer in college I might never have gone to the opera at all. But I did date a singer. Two of them, actually: a girl and a boy—or a soprano and a baritone, to be exact. She was the last girl I dated, back in my Columbia days, when my sexuality was more fluid than it is now. I adored her, Christina. Still do. But when Benjamin Hickok came along, I realized I was destined to find my authentic life in a man's embrace.

I always knew I was attracted to boys, but before Benjamin I maintained a "so what?" attitude. I was a little late coming to the realization that I could be a gay man and build a satisfying life in the process. When Ben swept me off my feet there was no turning back. I craved his kiss, his scent, his skin, his hands on my body. His very maleness filled my senses. And the fact that he had the most beautiful dick I've ever known only enhanced the experience.

Chris was stoic. Really, what do you do when your boyfriend tells you he's gay? There must be several scenarios, but Chris wished me luck and prepared to disappear from my life. I refused that approach to the future. I still loved Chris every bit as much as I had before I realized we wouldn't be fucking anymore. I wanted our friendship to continue. She took a little time off from our relationship, and then one day she phoned me and said, "Jules, I'll never forgive you 100% for what you did to me, but I think you're right. I think we should continue to be friends. I don't want to lose you just because you're a miserable son of a bitch. All men are. Why should I expect you to be different?"

"There's a *less* miserable son of a bitch out there with your name on his tag," I said, "but until he surfaces—and forever after—you have my devotion. It's a given." Chris and I had gone out to concerts occasionally, but with Benjamin I began to attend recitals, rehearsals, and opera performances—in earnest. Lincoln Center is a straight shot down Broadway from the tiny student apartment we shared. There was a lot going on, then as now. But City Opera was still running a full season in the State Theater back then, and that's where we were more likely to see Ben's colleagues and acquaintances in performance—rather than at the Met. And in the process I started to cut my music teeth. Did I even flirt with the notion of becoming a singer myself? Only briefly. Mercifully.

Ben and I had two good years together—I'd even call them great years—before graduation and his chance to study in London. I wouldn't have tried to stand in his way, even if I could have kept Ben at my side. We parted on loving terms. I cried a lot. He did, too. I still cry a little—but very little—when something reminds me of the lovely time we shared a decade-and-a-half ago. I'd only seen Ben twice in all those years. His concert career in Europe kept him busy. And he had to face the fact that his voice—though glorious—is not *quite* big enough to fill the Met. And the Met is now the only real opera game in town.

Ben gave a couple of concerts in New York, and I loved the chances to see him. A late supper after the concert was a reasonably safe situation for my heart. I could sit across a table from Ben for an hour or two and bask in the glow of his smile. I could kiss him good-bye and then head home without him. I could do it. I didn't happen to like it, but I could do it. Because that's all that was available to me. And I preferred it to not seeing him at all.

I dated dozens of men after Ben left New York. Nice men. Handsome men. Hot men. And I do love sex. I can find it, pretty much whenever I feel the need. But whether they were quick pickups or guys who shared their full names, never once did I find a man I wanted to get serious about. Only a few guys ever shared such great sex with me that I'd even wanted them to sleep over—in my bed. But in the clear morning light I always realized that they were most certainly *not* Ben. And that was that.

Chapter Two

I went to work that next morning—after the dreary *AÏDA*—just as I normally do on weekdays. The current project was an ad campaign for a fashion house, and they wanted me to show up to work on it—in house. It was mostly about photography, but the ad company hired me to add an "artistic flourish." They wanted classy. I gave it to them. I'm good at what I do. And I can always get work. Thank God.

At lunchtime I phoned Stuart to thank him again for coming to my aid when I was flat on my back on a New York City street—which is most assuredly *not* where I like to be flat on my back. Stuart took my call, to my great pleasure. I thanked him, of course, and then I asked if he would have dinner with me, maybe on the weekend. I was delighted that he said, "Yes." We set a time. I asked what he likes to eat, and he said, "Everything." So we decided I would choose a restaurant and text him the address. Done.

Had I just made date with a hot guy who might very well end up in my bed? Or was I satisfying an obligation? I couldn't be sure. But whatever I had just done, it was definitely the highlight of my day. I finished some work, but my brain also danced through several variations on the theme of dinner date: Would we meet at a French restaurant and enjoy soft lighting and romantic glances? Would we pig out on Happy Hour oysters and then float to my bed to test their effects on the male libido? Would we share a plate of pasta and end up on opposite ends of a strand of spaghetti? Or would we meet for sushi and then bow crisply—and repeatedly—as we said good night?

I was hoping for a version of our dinner date that leaned in the direction of romance. But I know better than to harbor overexpectations. I booked a table for two for Saturday at 7:00 at my favorite "new American," whatever that means.   I knew we'd get interesting food, and I knew the host—also interesting—would make a fuss over Stuart and make him feel entirely welcome (while I felt proud to be dining with such a handsome young man). And then I put the whole thing out of my mind. Mostly.

Chris and I met Thursday evening at our favorite Chinatown eatery. Salt-and-pepper softshell crab (the first of the season), eel in hot oil. Like that. Wonderful flavors and textures. I told Chris about my Saturday plans. Of course. I tell her everything. Nearly. She said, "Jules, really. I'm sure Stuart's very nice, and for all I know he's the hottest young tenor of his generation, but what's that to do with you?"

"Nothing whatsoever," I said. "It's dinner, dear. Not a marriage contract. Won't you let me have a little lightness, here and there?"

"I want you to have all the lightness you can stand—short of levitation—but I also want to see you grounded in reality," Chris said.

"Thank you for your concern, Chris, but I'm only having dinner with the nice young man who saved my life."

"Reality, Jules."

"Very well, Chris. I'm only going to dinner with the guy who helped me up after I was hit by a cab in front of Lincoln Center. Is that pedestrian enough for you?"

"Quite," she said.

"And could we change the subject?" I asked. "You haven't told me a thing about the music festival in Austria next summer. So what are you singing?"

"Concert arias, mostly. Mozart and Bellini. Standard stuff. Beautiful. Fun to sing. I'm looking forward to it, even though there are no particular challenges. I don't know if I told you, but there's also a concert performance of *COSÌ* for the summer festival in Prague. I don't know the whole cast, but Rebecca is doing it with me." Rebecca Cathcart is a friend of ours—a mezzo with an extraordinary instrument and a wicked sense of humor. I predict she'll be the Met's next great Carmen. But we'll see. Rebecca's agent discovered her singing in the choir at the Mt. Zion AME Church in Harlem. He offered her just the direction she needed to launch a career. Rebecca is a delight to hear and a delight to know.

Chris said, "I just found out the baritone will be Ben. I thought you should know. Maybe you'll want to come and hear us. Prague is beautiful in July. And I know *COSÌ* is a favorite of yours. Think about it."

"I'm sure it will be lovely, but I don't think so, Chris. I don't think I could do it. I haven't heard Ben sing in five years, anyway. I don't know how I'd deal with seeing him again, at this point. I've ripped off the scab so many times, I don't know if my heart will ever heal." Chris was understanding. She's a remarkable woman, and a remarkable singer. Chris hasn't had all her professional hopes fulfilled yet. But she's sung at the Met—The Queen of the Night in *DIE ZAUBERFLÖTE*, mostly. I asked Chris once, "How the fuck can you get through a performance like that?"

She said, "I have to know exactly what I'm doing. I have to be certain of every note. Every phrase. But when I walk on stage, I have to just do it, without thinking too much. Overthinking kills the moment. And it interferes with the music. And it's always about the music. If I'm not swept away by the music, then you won't be either." I decided that was as clear an explanation of the process as any.

That Thursday night we ate too much exceptionally good food, drank Chinese beer, and then hopped on an uptown 6 train with a contented buzz in our heads. We got off at 68th Street, and I walked Chris west to her building. "Thanks for a lovely evening, Jules," she said. "And do be careful."

"Oh, I know dear. I have five whole blocks to walk to get myself home. But I think I can handle it," I said.

"That's not what I meant, and you know it," she said. "Call me on Sunday."

"Will do. Sleep well." And I headed home. The cool night air was refreshing. I made it home without incident. I got myself ready for bed. But instead of conking out, I lay there thinking of Stuart: His face. His strong hands. The beautiful body I assumed lay beneath his clothing. "Enough!" I told myself. I only indulged in my excess for a few more minutes before sleep claimed me.

Stuart and I arrived at the restaurant almost simultaneously. The attentive host seated us and gave me an approving nod. Stuart was even handsomer than I remembered, I decided. And I figured the lighting was probably making *me* look *my* best, too. That was a reassuring thought. We ordered food and wine. I'm always more comfortable once the choices are made. I relaxed into getting-to-know-you mode. "Where did you grow up?" I asked. Might as well start at the beginning.

"In Chicago, or just north of it. My parents are instructors at Northwestern, in Evanston. They both teach music. So I'm following the family business. What about you?" Stuart asked.

"I grew up in Connecticut. Nice enough, most of it, but boring." That was not strictly the truth, but close enough for a first date. "So for college I was ready for the big city. That's why I chose Columbia. And I've been here ever since. I know you're a tenor, and that you're learning Radamès, but what else do you sing?"

"I've only learned a few roles so far—and lots of *lieder*—but I'm starting to get work. Last year I sang Roméo in Hamburg. Gounod's R & J is very popular right now. And this fall I sang Alfredo in Venice. It's my hands-down favorite." It's one of mine, too, which made me wonder yet again how the same composer could have created the sublime *TRAVIATA* and the ridiculous *AÏDA*. I snapped out of stupid speculations and concentrated on my guest.

"It sounds like you're on your way," I said.

"I hope so. Singing is all I've ever wanted."

All he's ever wanted? Sounds a bit limited, I thought. But what I said was, "Even so, I'll bet the dessert list will tempt you." We ordered. And while we awaited the appearance of our sweets, I said, "You know, we could go to my place for coffee and a nightcap. If you like. It's only a few blocks from here," I said.

"Thanks, Julian. I'd like that," Stuart said. And that's what we did. As we walked to my apartment, I didn't feel easy enough to put my arm around Stuart. But we walked slowly and so close together that my hand brushed his occasionally. Deliberately? Maybe. We arrived, and I let us in.

I have an open kitchen. I took Stuart's jacket and suggested he sit at the counter. I went into the kitchen to make coffee. I sensed that Stuart was watching me intently as I went about the business of grinding beans and brewing two espressos. I poured two glasses of cognac. I served our drinks and then came around the counter and stood next to Stuart. He leaned comfortably into the kitchen space, and I leaned determinedly into *his* space. Our lips met. I had no real idea of what to expect. But he kissed me! "That was nice," I said.

"Yes."

"I want more," I said.

"So do I," he said. I kissed Stuart again. And again. We blushed a little—both of us, I think. I sensed that Stuart would have been happy to jump into bed and have at it. But I was in no hurry. I didn't want to miss anything. I removed Stuart's shirt and draped it over the back of the barstool next. His skin was velvety, his shoulders were broad and strong, and his chest was delicate, almost like a boy's. I encouraged Stuart to stand so I could drop his nice wool trousers. And then his shorts, too.

"Jesus!" I exclaimed.

"What's wrong?" he asked.

"Not a bloody thing," I said. "You're so beautiful I don't know where to start."

"Just start," he suggested.

"Good thinking," I said. I knelt at Stuart's feet and removed his shoes and socks, and then his slacks and shorts. I couldn't resist kissing his feet, which were just as strong and generous as his hands. But I dared not linger there for long, with all the other discovery to come. I slipped out of my clothes and put them aside. And then we faced each other in full birthday. Our bodies looked to me like a perfect fit. I offered Stuart my hand. He took it in his, and I led him to my bed.

I think Stuart would have been content with a quickie. I slowed him down. I took my time exploring every surface, every texture, every curve. I hadn't tasted anyone so inviting in a long time. Fifteen years, to be exact. Stuart's skin was as soft as a baby's. His dick, however, was all about manhood. Every part of him seemed delicious.

When I indicated that I wanted Stuart to roll over, he complied with perfect obedience. And it was at that moment I realized he had the most perfect ass I'd ever seen. Even Benjamin is not so finely made. *But never mind Ben,* I thought. *He* wasn't in my bed, and Stuart *was.* I dove my face between Stuart's legs and feasted, as if I had been starved for a very long time. As, indeed, I had been. I didn't want to leave that position. Stuart seemed content with it, too. But my dick called to me, and it's hard to ignore that call.

I sat back on my heels and spread Stuart's legs very slightly, very gently. Again he was obedient. And then I mounted him. I took my time. I held Stuart's head and kissed him tenderly. When I presented my dick—carefully, slowly—he received it. I stopped his gasp with a kiss. "Are you okay?" I asked.

"Yes," he said. "Don't stop."

That was all the spur I needed. I proceeded to move inside Stuart with great care. I had no idea what he wanted, what he liked. So I simply inhabited him with respect and tenderness. How long was I there? I don't have a clue about those things. I plumbed Stuart's depths as long as I could before I erupted with a loud shout. I'm not usually very vocal in bed. That night I was. Stuart was quiet. When our breathing returned to normal, I slid away and encouraged Stuart to roll over on his side, so I could see him better. He started to chuckle.

"I came, too," Stuart said. And sure enough, there was a great puddle of Stuart's essence in the middle of my bed. I dove for it, to see what I could taste before it all soaked into the bedclothes. Stuart said, "I've never done that before."

I was stunned. Virginity was not a concept I had considered in a lot of years. I had been eager to lose mine. And when I was sixteen and a boy my age wanted to take it, I surrendered it gladly. The pain was even more than I expected. But nothing I couldn't handle. And I never looked back. "Are you okay with it?" I asked.

"Yes," he said. "I've thought about it, and I've fooled around with a few guys. But I'm sort of engaged to my high school sweetheart. And I always thought we would marry and live together, here.

She's in Evanston and I'm in New York, mostly, so it's complicated. But I thought it was just a matter of time. And yet, I see so many hot guys who make me wonder about my choices."

"That's New York for you," I said.

"And speaking of hot guys," Stuart said, "Julian, that was amazing."

"I agree," I said. "Look, Stuart, there's no pressure here. If you want to revisit my bed sometime, I'd like it very much. And if not, then that's your choice. But I like you—very much—and I hope we can be friends, whichever way it goes."

"Yes. Friends. I don't have many friends. I think I used to, in school and all. But these days I'm travelling so much. There's hardly anyone to see when I get back to New York. I'd like knowing I can see you, Julian."

"That's a given. And meanwhile, since you're not traveling tonight, could I have another kiss?"

"Of course," Stuart said. He fell back into my arms and gave me another of his warm, wet kisses. And then he developed an interest in my nipples, and then my armpits. And soon he was working his way slowly to my groin, which sprang back into ready mode. I don't usually get too interested in receiving a blowjob. I usually prefer to be *doing* something. But Stuart was so focused on my dick that I let him explore it. And he proceeded to offer me full attention. Full honors. And I rewarded him with the finest load I had to offer.

It was only fair of Stuart to gift *me* in kind. He scooted up my body and straddled my shoulders. It gave me the chance to revisit that amazing ass of his, with both hands. Stuart rested his pretty balls on my chest and worked his handsome dick until he creamed all over my face. We laughed and tasted and kissed and laughed some more. It was delightful.

After we came down from our coital high, I said, "Speaking of not traveling tonight, will you stay over? This bed is plenty big enough for two, as you know."

"I shouldn't," Stuart said. "I'm flying on Monday, and there's always so much to do before a trip. But, yes, I will."

"Good," I said. "I'll help you get ready for your trip. You can have my whole Sunday if you want it. I'm very practical. Very efficient."

"If you're as efficient at packing as you are at fucking, then I'm sure I have nothing to worry about. Consider it a date." We washed-up a little and brushed our teeth. I keep a guest toothbrush in the bathroom. Doesn't everyone? That was all Stuart needed to get himself ready for sleep. It wasn't as if he needed pajamas, or anything like them. He headed back to the bedroom and settled into my bed. I turned out lights, double-checked the front door lock, and then joined him. There were kisses, of course. I wasn't entirely ready to let go of Stuart. He seemed to feel the same about me. But eventually my bed was all stillness.

Just before I drifted off to sleep—with a lovely young man snoring softly beside me—I said to myself, "Julian, what the fuck are you doing? Are you trying to fall in love with a straight boy? Are you planning to give your heart to a man who doesn't want it? Ben loved you. Still does, most likely. If he weren't working in Europe he'd be by your side. Most likely. This one? Nice boy. Wonderful ass. Best case scenario? He'll meet some beauty who turns his head and he'll be off with her. Worst case scenario? He'll decide his sexual ambiguity is all your fault, and he'll hate you for it. And he is a singer, after all. If he's any good, he'll probably end up on the road 350 days a year. Julian, grow up!"

Did I listen? Did I take my own best advice? Not really. Instead, I snuggled down into the bedclothes and savored the warmth beside me.

Chapter Three

We woke late the next morning. I went to the kitchen to make coffee. When Stuart wandered in and sat at the counter, I looked at him and said, "Good morning, bedhead. You look edible."

"You're not so bad yourself," he said. "What would a guy have to do to get a T-shirt?" he asked.

"I normally keep my boys naked, but I might be persuaded. If your kiss is good enough," I said.

"With morning breath?"

"That's a prerequisite."

"Then exact your price, sir," Stuart said. I went to him, embraced him, and he kissed me so warmly that my head began to swim.

"Jesus, Julian!" I said to myself. "You're in way over your head. Those are forever thoughts creeping into your brain, in case you hadn't noticed. This will never do." I tried to keep it light. I went to my closet for Ts and sandals for both of us. I served coffee with hot milk. I toasted a bagel from the freezer and served it with good butter, just so we'd have a little something in our stomachs. "I think we should slip on the same clothes we wore last night—that way we're equal—and head out to The Smith or someplace for brunch," I said. "And then we can get on with your day. You didn't want a shower this morning, did you?" I asked.

"Hate them," Stuart said. "They take too long."

"Exactly," I said. "And I like my men natural. Speaking of which, I'd be content to spend the rest of the day in bed, coming up for air and food deliveries every now and then. But. Let's be practical, as I promised. What do you need for your trip? Do you have a list?"

"I do, actually," Stuart said. "Mostly I need some of those terrible travel-sized toiletries. And a new little toiletry kit. The old one from school fell apart. Some new shorts would be good. And socks."

"Did you put tissue paper on your list?" I asked.

"Tissue paper?" he asked.

"Oh, Stuart," I said. "I'm about to share a secret imparted to me years ago by a wise old Gypsy. You'll never pack your bags the same way again."

"I'm thinking maybe there are lots of things I'll never do the same way again," Stuart said.

"That's not necessarily a bad thing," I said. "We should probably head out, but could I just have you in my bed for five minutes before we go? No, ten minutes. No, twenty minutes. Yes, that's perfect. Will you give me twenty minutes of *you* before we go?"

"Yes," Stuart said. And we headed for the bedroom, slipped off our Ts and sandals, and fell back into bed. It was one of the best ideas of my life, I thought at the time, that last twenty minutes. It gave me a reason to believe that the events of the evening before were real. Stuart mirrored—or seemed to mirror—every desire of mine. All my longing for him. All my passion.

I kept my word, making certain we resurfaced after twenty minutes. "How long will you be away?" I asked, as we were dressing.

"Six weeks, this trip."

"My, my. Six weeks. I was hoping for *one*. But, it is what it is. Do you have international cell phone service?" I asked.

"No," he said, "but if *you* do, then I think I can receive texts and calls without crazy charges. I'd like to hear from you. I'll miss you, Julian. Very much."

"Please don't fuck with me, Stuart," I said. "Please don't reach for my heart if you don't want it." Stuart lunged forward and embraced me.

"I never wanted another man's heart," he said. "But I want yours. And you have mine. Julian, you have my heart. I'll put it on a chain for you, if you like. But? I don't know what that means. I don't know what I have to share—what I can give you. I'm not going to spend the rest of my life in your beautiful bed, as much as I might want to. I just don't know. I don't know much of anything. I don't know if I can go back to Evanston and marry my fiancée. I don't know if I can build a major career. But I *do* know I can sing. And that's my focus. And if you can accept that, then I'll give you everything I can. I'm a tenor. I'm supposed to know about passion and drama, but mostly from the music. And now you're making me feel it. I think I'm ready. For what it's worth."

I had no words. I kissed him, and then we headed for the door and the real world. I liked Stuart in daylight even more than in the soft glow of nighttime. He requires no artifice, no enhancement to be effortlessly appealing. I realized that Stuart's eyes were intensely green, with all the depth and fire of priceless emeralds. I admired his Adam's apple, and the little dip just above his collar bone, and the tiny mole on his right cheek. I felt dreamy about the whole package, really. I felt wonderful. I also felt terrified.

We brunched, and laughed, and spent long moments simply gazing into each other's eyes. I have no memory of what we ate. I only remember Stuart. And afterward we did his shopping—at Bloomingdale's and Duane Reade. It was all so romantic, even choosing socks whose tops won't restrict blood flow—not an easy task these days. And then we took our haul to Stuart's small Westside apartment.

He had two suitcases—one medium-sized and one small—open and ready on his bed. He seemed to know exactly how many suits, which shoes, and how many jeans he needed. He'd obviously done this before. I opened the tissue paper and showed Stuart how to wrap not just shoes—so they don't get the clothes dirty—but also clothing—so it doesn't wrinkle. "See what you think when you unpack," I said. "I expect you'll be hooked."

"I already am," Stuart said, and he kissed me. I had done everything I promised, and it was time for me to leave. I didn't want to, of course. With the packing finished, Stuart's bed was now unencumbered. Available. I'd have been delighted to sink into it with him. But it wasn't fair. He needed the rest of the evening alone to prepare himself for an early morning flight and everything that would follow it.

"Thank you for a memorable weekend," I said.

"Thank *you* for your help, and for agreeing to be my friend. And for accepting my heart. I think I'm leaving it in good hands," Stuart said.

"I'll try to prove worthy of it," I said.

"You already have," he said. "And you'll text me once in a while?

"Of course," I said. I never liked good-byes, and this one was starting to upset me in the extreme. I put a cap on it. I reached out and touched Stuart's cheek. I looked into his beautiful eyes. Briefly. And then I was out the door. When I got to the street I walked for a while. I knew where I was—more or less. I decided to head uptown for a dozen blocks or so and then get on a crosstown bus, going through Central Park. I was in no hurry.

When I got home I stripped off the clothes I had been wearing—on and off—since the evening before. I could smell Stuart on those clothes and on my body. I hated to lose his scent, but even I knew it was time to move on. I put my clothes in laundry bags—sorted by washing, shirts, and dry- cleaning— and I took a hot shower.

When I emerged from the bathroom, I was feeling ready to face a phone call to Chris. And I was also feeling ready to face a bite of supper. I suggested she join me. I apologized for the short notice. "Sorry, love," she said, "but I had a huge lunch with Re- becca, and I have an early rehearsal. So, I'm in for the night. How are you?"

"Don't ask," I said.

"I just did," Chris said.

"Besides besotted? Just dandy," I said. "I think you'll be pleased to know Stuart will be in Europe for the next six weeks."

"So, you think I want to watch you pine away for six weeks? You think I want to see you in pain? How dare you, Jules! Is that who you think I am?"

"Please don't jump on me, Chris," I said. "I feel bad enough as it is. A rebuke from you is more than I'm prepared to deal with just now."

"Relax, dear. The last thing I want is to abuse you. Are you free on Tuesday evening?"

"I think so," I said.

"Good," Chris said. "I'll cook for you. Why don't you bring a baguette and one of those little ripened cheeses from that shop near you? I have plenty of wine in the house."

"You're too good to me," I said.

"Yes, but we know that. Just get your ass over here on Tuesday evening, and we'll sort everything out." Talking to Chris made me feel a little better. I ordered a small pizza and prepared to hunker down for the night. I would be just fine. Wouldn't I?

Chapter Four

Isn't it great to have work to do? I've sometimes wondered what retired people do—why they want to get out of bed. Monday morning arrived on schedule. While I was having coffee, I imagined that Stuart must be half way to Frankfurt. I went to my desk and took up the project at hand: I had accepted a commission to illustrate a series of children's books. At first I worried that the stories might be too saccharine for my taste and talent. But my agent assured me the author has a rather dark, almost edgy view of childhood, complete with boogeymen and monsters.

I read the first story, and I was hooked. I jumped right in and gave it all my own childhood darkness. The author said it was perfect. We worked our way through the first three stories. That April morning, I got on with book four and then put it aside in favor of some newer things that needed my attention. I don't usually have what you'd call lunch. But that Monday I decided I had earned a little treat—a small diversion to soften the empty ache in my heart—what there was of it. I threw on some clothes and ran a brush through my hair. Close enough, I decided, looking in the mirror. And I headed out.

The little *taverna* in the next block is welcoming, but the food can be a bit uneven. I studied the fish on ice in the front window. There was a small porgy that sparkled as if it had been caught that morning. I walked in, and one of the servers smiled and gestured to suggest a table for me. I waited until he was free to approach me, so I could take him to the fish display and show him my choice. He signaled the grill man, and we were all set. I sat, ordered an eggplant salad thing to start—I must have that in Greek or Turkish restaurants—and a carafe of *retsina*. Dining alone is not my favorite pastime. That Monday afternoon I was resigned to a solitary meal. But a quality meal.

The eggplant salad was too cold, of course. It always is. But I never really mind that. The porgy was perfectly grilled, with nothing more than some olive oil and a sprig of oregano and a garlic clove in the cavity. After a spritz of lemon, the only thing that could have improved it would have been Stuart across the table to share it with me. I didn't dwell on it. I knew that for at least the next six weeks—and most likely for the rest of my life—I would not have Stuart across the table from me. I knew it. But I didn't have to like it.

I don't take Greek coffee very often. I made an exception that day. "Not too sweet," I requested. The waiter also brought me a little pastry. Speaking of sweet. I ate it. And the coffee was actually quite nice. It was a lovely luncheon. I left the restaurant feeling fortified and nearly ebullient. And then I went back to my apartment and did what all sensible people do after lunch—I took a nap. It was an excellent choice.

When I got out of bed and went back to my desk, I was able to make some decisions about projects that had been confusing me. It all seemed so obvious. The work flowed. I did what needed to be done, at that particular time, and then I decided to take the rest of the day off. Some leftovers for supper, and a late movie on TCM. It was a day well spent. One day down. How many to go?

Chris's apartment is warmly inviting. I always thought it's the perfect combination of spare and *gemütlich*. She obviously admires fine things, but she also keeps clutter to a minimum. And—to my knowledge—she hasn't a stick of furniture that is not perfectly suited to the human body. I love being there. There were some weeks, a dozen years before, when I camped out for a while: sleeping on Chris's sofa, scrambling some eggs, and eating them while watching the morning game shows and drinking coffee generously laced with Scotch.

Chris dealt with that period in my life—after Ben left New York—with the same grace as she's dealt with all the years of our friendship: She's always known when to apply a cold compress to my fevered brow and when to administer a swift kick in the ass. I can't see how I'd have survived my adulthood— such as it is—without her. That Tuesday evening was no exception.

Chris was always a better cook than I am. She gets it—how to combine flavors and textures and how to patiently make a dish happen the way it should happen. She steamed mussels for us, in white wine with aromatics and a touch of chopped fresh tomato. Chris served the mussels with crusty toasts that she rubbed with garlic and anointed with olive oil. Perfect.

For our next course she grilled pork tenderloin until it was nicely seared but still pink inside. Also perfect. Salad. Fresh fruit with the cheese I brought. Over coffee, Chris said, "Jules, you've told me nothing about what's going on. I can't be much of a friend to you if you leave me in the dark."

"Of course," I said. "We had dinner Saturday at East Pole. The host made a big fuss over Stuart, of course. It was fun. And then we went to my place for coffee and a cognac, and I kissed him. And he kissed me back. And then he came to my bed, where I made love to him and he responded totally. Chris, it was amazing. I'm still reeling from it. By morning—over a toasted bagel—I knew I was hooked.

"Stuart told me some things about himself, like about his fiancée back home in Chicago. He also told me he loves me, but that he doesn't know what he has to offer, considering that the most important thing in his life is his career."

"How good do you think he is?" Chris asked. "That may sound frivolous, but I think it matters."

"Yes, well, I've never heard his voice, but he sang Roméo last summer in Hamburg."

"Impressive."

"And Alfredo last fall in Venice."

"Also impressive," Chris said. "What if he's poised to become the next Pavarotti? What if his career consumes most of his energy, and nearly all of his time? What does that leave you?

"Thank you, dear, for going right to the meat of things," I said.

"There's no sense in pretending, dear. Jules, what do you want?" Chris asked.

"I want Stuart. But I don't want his baggage. I don't want his fiancée. I don't want his unavailability. I don't want anything that comes between us. Does that make me a bad person?"

"Could we talk about availability? Jules, I would have transformed myself into a *hausfrau* if you had been available. But there was no decision for me to make. You decided for me. And I think you have another decision to make as well."

"I suppose I'll have to end this thing. I can't see any other way."

"Now what?" she asked. "You're an honorable man. More or less. What are you going to do about Stuart? You said he loves you. I believe you. And? How will you handle that?"

"Chris, he gave me his heart. He offered to put it on a chain. I feel like I'm wearing it right now. How could I just give it back?"

"Ouch!" Chris said. "I don't envy your situation. But there's nothing you have to do tonight—or tomorrow, for that matter. It's not like you have to send him a Dear Stuart text in the next six weeks. As long as you know—really know, deep in your heart—that this relationship is unfair to both of you, then I think you'll take care of it when you see him again. Does that make sense?"

"It does, actually," I said. "Thanks, Chris, as always."

"They'll give you my bill at the desk on your way out. Speaking of which . . ."

"I was just leaving. When is our next opera?" I asked.

"Two weeks, I think. And that should be the last of the season."

"Will you have dinner with me on the weekend?"

"Yes. I'll call you tomorrow," Chris said. "Get some shut-eye, sailor."

"Aye, aye, Captain," I said. I gave Chris a good-night kiss and headed home. Did I feel a bit better? Yes, actually. I had decided. And while I didn't write my decision in stone, I did write it in my heart: I would have to give Stuart up—for his sake and mine. I would have to figure out the kindest way to do it, for both of us. But not right away. Surely I could savor my romantic fantasy a bit longer. Couldn't I?

Chapter Five

Spring seemed to have a vise grip on the city. Flowering trees were in full bloom. Window boxes and tree boxes were bursting with tulips and daffodils. It was glorious, despite the incidence of sneezing and watery eyes among the human population. Trees all over the city—even the ones without blossoms—began to sport new little pale green leaf buds. My sap was rising, too. And I wasn't the only Narcissus displaying himself in public. Hot guys seemed to be everywhere—and happy to throw off heavy winter wrappings in favor of lighter, more revealing attire. By mid-summer I'm always complaining loudly about the heat, but the first warm days in May always bring gladness to my heart.

One afternoon I was headed downtown on the 6 Train to get some art supplies. There was an interesting guy in the same car. I'd call him a muscle daddy, with a shaved head. We exchanged looks—not smiles, exactly. More like stares. At the station stops, he moved closer to me. At 42nd Street, he stood next to me and said, "Nice ass."

"Thanks."

"I want to fuck it."

"Okay."

"Get off with me at 14th Street."

"Okay." And I did. There was no conversation. I followed him for about three blocks to a small walk-up building. We went into his apartment, and he showed me his bed and told me to strip and then get into it face-down. I was entirely obedient. He stripped too, so I was able to see that I was about to receive a huge dick—a *beyond*-huge dick. It seemed too late to rethink any of it. I did as I was told. I accepted the consequences.

He lubed us both—mercifully—and then he shoved that monster dick of his up my ass. I was silent. I was resolved. I wasn't certain I had actually made my bed, but I was certainly lying in it. I accepted him, thrust after thrust. I couldn't quite enjoy it—because the pain made that at least 50% out of the question—so I decided to find some edification in it. I thought, *For my sins. For my most grievous sins. Let me here do penance. Let this act absolve me from all my bad choices, all my transgressions. Let this wash me clean.*

My new muscle daddy pounded me for as long as he needed to. And then he announced his climax with the usual heavy breathing and rapid strokes, plus the exclamation, "Jesus Fucking Christ!" I was silent. I accepted his gift. It wasn't what I'd have chosen, but I've learned that men give what they can. And this one had just given me his best. I knew that. When he softened his posture and lay on top of me with his full weight, I relaxed into the pressure of his body on mine. And when a few drops of sweat or tears fell onto my face, I welcomed them.

We lay there for a while, and then he got up and offered me his hand to pull me up from his bed and into his very strong arms. He embraced me sweetly, and he kissed me for the first time. "I'm Van," he said.

"Jules," I said.

"I'm just going to make a pot of tea. Will you join me?" I would have preferred a stiff drink, but I accepted tea. Van indicated his little dining table for me, and he went into his kitchen, filled the kettle, and put it on the stove. I sat on a chair with a black leather seat. Very comfortable. While the water was heating Van brought out cups and spoons; napkins and a sugar bowl; a small pitcher of milk, and some cookies on a little blue-and-white plate. I waited patiently, using the time to look around Van's apartment. It looked strong and totally neat—like the man. The only visible curlicues in the room were the handles of the silver tea-strainer that was resting on my cup.

When the tea was made, Van brought the pot to the table and sat opposite me. "Three minutes," he said, and he smiled easily. I returned his smile. I also studied the man before me who had been merely a focused fucking machine only a few minutes before. I decided that he was quite handsome—built, but not excessively so. His nipples were generous and pink. I wanted to suck them, and other body parts, too. I wondered what it would be like to make love to Van, to explore his entire body. I wondered if his taste in sex would permit it. All this speculation produced a raging hard-on. I was a bit embarrassed and pleased that the table was hiding my lower body from view.

"Nice place," I said.

"Thanks," he said. "I've lived here more than ten years now. Time flies."

"Tell me," I said. "I'm an illustrator. What do you do?"

"I'm an advocate for children in the shelter system. My schedule depends on the court's schedule, so that's why I'm off this afternoon. Most of the time I'm in Family Court. The kids need all the support they can get."

"I'll bet," I said. "I thought maybe you were an iron worker, or something really macho like that."

"Because of before?" Van asked, indulgently, indicating the bedroom. "That's just sex. Life is different."

I wasn't so sure. I always thought of people as totalities. I don't think I have compartments. Van obviously did. "Thanks for having me over," I said. "That was—quite an experience."

"Thanks for being here. I like you, Jules. I'd like to see you again."

"Sure," I said. What else could I say? I wanted to see Van again, too, but I wasn't certain my ass could survive a repeat performance. And I didn't know how to ask for something gentler. So I let it go. We exchanged phone numbers. I washed up a little and put my clothes back on. Van was still gloriously naked as he walked me to the door. He kissed me tenderly. I could feel his amazing dick beginning to stand at attention again—mirroring mine. "Could we maybe get together and just kiss sometime?" I asked.

"Sure," Van said. "I love to kiss." He also seemed to like kneading my buttocks with his large, strong hands. It felt great, but it also reminded me of what came before. And I didn't know if I could go there again. As I was headed down the stairs to the street, I winced with pain a few times when I moved too quickly. I had checked carefully when I was in Van's bathroom. There was no blood, so I knew I was fine. It would just take a few days until I felt whole again. I wasn't worried.

I was more saddened, to think that such a beautiful, quality man had such intense needs for anonymity and domination. I couldn't think of Van as violent, exactly. He had done me no real harm, after all. But I wondered if I could ever really trust such a man. I wondered if he would call me or text me. I assumed I would not contact him. But if he did reach out, would I see him again? Would I decide a chance to experience his kiss and his body again— his nipples alone were worthy of a lengthy visit— would outweigh the risks? Probably. Would that be wise?

I walked back to Union Square and then down 4th Avenue to the art supply house. I bought the paints and papers I needed, and then headed home. On the way I wondered if Chris was right—that I had been engaging in risky behavior of late.

Van did phone me—the next week. He said, "I was telling my friend Michael about you, and he wants to meet you. Why don't you come here some evening and I'll cook for you? What about this Friday? Sorry, Jules, I almost forgot! Michael and I have tickets for a concert at Carnegie Hall on Friday night. What about Saturday? Would that work for you?" I was too stunned to reply sensibly. Instead I hemmed and hawed about some up-in-the-air weekend plans. And could I maybe get back to him tomorrow? He agreed. We hung up.

"Jules, what are you doing?" I asked myself. "Some horse-dicked power-lifter you met on the subway wants you to meet his friend—maybe another horse-dicked power-lifter—for dinner and God knows what else in the bedroom. And you're considering it? What's your problem?" Well, of course, my problem was that I was lonely and feeling guilty about the Stuart thing. And of course there was also the fact that Van was a perfectly nice man. And there was no real reason for me to avoid him. Hadn't I already made it clear that I was interested in more vanilla, more romantic pursuits? Hadn't he agreed to my terms?

The next afternoon I phoned Van and accepted his invitation. "Come early," Van suggested. "About 6:00. We can take a bottle of wine up to the roof and enjoy the sunset—weather permitting. I'll make something that's easy to serve whenever we're ready for dinner. You'll like Michael. He's a charmer." I thanked Van for the invitation. I decided it would be a very pleasant, very easy evening, plus a chance to meet another interesting man. And whatever happened, I could take care of myself, after all. Couldn't I?

Chapter Six

It was a busy work week, with two project deadlines. It didn't give me much time to think about Van, luckily. Had I been free to fret about him I might have changed my mind and cancelled. Instead, I simply got on with my life. By Saturday morning it was too late to back out without being really rude, and that was never my intention. I was resigned. I was cheerful. I organized a few things on my desk, and then it was time to get ready and head out. On my way to Van's I stopped at my favorite chocolatier for something to take along as a little host gift. The situation was all very unremarkable— except for the chocolates, which were extraordinary.

Van greeted me with an embrace and a kiss. So far so good. "Julian Harcourt, meet Michael Fernandez." I greeted a handsome man about our age. He looked really fit and strong without being overly pumped. In fact, he looked a bit like Van but with an olive cast to his skin and lots of wavy black hair. I liked his smile. I liked his handshake. I quite liked *him.* I relaxed for the first time all day. Van thanked me for the chocolates and said, "It looks like the weather is holding. Shall we give the roof a try?"

Michael and I agreed, so Van handed Michael some glasses and napkins. He gave me a plate of little toasts with slices of country pâté on them. Cornichons on the side. He grabbed a bottle of wine and a corkscrew. And we were ready for the climb.

The sky was a bit gray when we stepped onto Van's roof, but the clouds soon blew away. It turned out to be a lovely evening. We drank wine and nibbled the canapés. Getting-to-know-you speak was easy and comfortable. "Michael's a wigmaker at Met Opera," Van said. "He does gorgeous work."

"I'm a devotee, as it happens," I said. "My friend Chris and I have had the same seats for the last five seasons. Actually, she's a singer as well as my best friend and opera buddy. Maybe you've dressed her: Christina Grimaldi."

"Of course," Michael said. "Nice lady. Terrific voice. I keep hoping she'll get more roles at the Met."

"So do I," I said. "So we have that in common for sure."

"I'll bet there's more."

"I wouldn't be surprised."

Van seemed pleased that Michael and I were hitting it off. "We haven't received our tickets for next season yet," he said.

"No, nor have we," I said. "But we'll have to trade schedules to see if we overlap. It's always fun to meet for a glass of champagne at intermission." The sunset was just reaching its full glory when the sky blackened and there was a sudden downpour as if the heavens had opened and dumped all their rain almost at once. It sent us scrambling for cover. The rain showed no signs of lifting, so Van said, "Let's go in. I can get the glasses tomorrow." We headed to Van's apartment and stripped off our wet clothes.

Van hung everything in the shower. It was a mess, but we laughed a lot and made the most of it.

Van brought out a towel for us to dry our hair (Michael's and my hair and Van's pate). Then Van reached for me and for Michael and brought the three of us together for a group kiss. It was so warm that any residual fears of mine all melted away. Van said, "We could go to table and start dinner, but we could also have dessert first." It seemed a shame to waste the situation: three naked, horny men locked in an embrace.

"Dessert, please," I said. Michael laughed easily, and we headed to Van's bed, the three of us landing with me in the middle. Michael and Van were comfortable old friends. I was the newbie. They focused their attention on me. They stroked me and petted me and kissed me. In fact, no matter what else was happening, I was rarely without a kiss from at least one of them. I didn't know exactly where we were headed, nor did I care. No one was in a rush. We were each committed explorers. I didn't want to miss any territory. Michael's body was even finer than I had imagined. I tried to experience it all. But there was Van's body to consider too!

I finally got my chance to investigate Van's nipples. He was lying on his back while I nibbled and suckled. He encouraged me to bite. I tried to comply. Safely. Van urged me on. And then he issued a command. "Get inside," he instructed, and he threw his legs over my shoulders. I did as I was told: I mounted him and presented my dick. "Do it," Van said. I pushed forward, carefully. He took me in, all the way. Van gasped slightly with my first tentative thrust, but after that his face took on a Zen-like composure.

And then I knew Michael was behind me. Even before he started to rim me, I knew he was there. And when he wrapped his arms fully around my body, I knew that his beautiful dick—proud and strong—was in place to enter me. I wanted it. Even if Michael's dick had been twice the size of Van's—which it was not, mercifully—I would have taken it. I would have taken anything Michael had to offer. And I did. Gladly. I had never been so blissfully sandwiched between two layers of perfect masculinity. And I feel certain I never will be again.

When the three of us had all played our roles in that little drama and then relaxed into a sweaty heap, Van said, "Well, I suppose I should see to dinner." We all laughed, of course. Van served us a delicious meal. The centerpiece was a remarkable lamb stew with little carrots and turnips and pearl onions and peas. The seasoning was just right. I was impressed. The other dishes—including the actual dessert—were perfectly matched. Over coffee, Van said, "You know, Michael is staying here tonight, and I went to Russ & Daughters for smoked salmon for our breakfast. There's more than enough for three, if you want to sleep over, Jules. I'd like it very much."

"And so would I," Michael said. "Very much. Please say yes."

"Your clothes may not be dry until morning any way," Van said. "It may not be safe for you to go out tonight."

"I know how to choose my fights," I said. "Of course I'll stay. Thank you. I don't think I snore any more than the average guy who's had too much wine to drink. But if I do, you can always kick me out of bed. I hear that sleeping on the floor is good for the back."

"No, that won't be necessary, I'm sure," Van said. "We have other remedies for snoring."

"Exactly," Michael said. "Without even trying I can think of at least a half dozen ways to stop your snoring. But I can also imagine loving the sound of it. Who knows?"

"You two are quite remarkable men," I said. "And remarkable friends. I feel honored to be included in this friendship."

"You did well with the initiation rites," Van said. "I think we can welcome you—Michael, do I have your yea?" Michael nodded. "Yes, I think we can welcome you into the Brotherhood of the Holy Phallus, with all the rights and privileges that attend your enrolment."

I have just enough of a flair for the dramatic to know when I've been fed a cue. I slipped from my chair and knelt at Van's feet. I put my forehead to the carpet and awaited further instructions. I think I got it right. Van stood and said, "Arise, Brother Julian." I sat back on my heels, and there was my head on a par with the holiest—or maybe *unholiest* phallus I had ever encountered. Van and Michael both lifted me up, embraced me, and said, in unison, "Go forth and conjugate."

"But not tonight," Michael said. "Tonight is just for the three of us. I'm going to pour us a Drambuie, if you don't mind, Van."

"Of course not," he said.

"Let's seal our bond with honey. Not that kisses need sweetening." And we did. Van brought out some robes. It was fun being naked through dinner, but the change in temperature after sundown had begun to creep into the apartment. It felt good to have a little cover. And it felt good to sit quietly with my new friends, enjoying their company. It all felt good. No one wanted to break the circle, but eventually we needed to return to Van's bed for sleeping. And that's what we did.

When we settled in, I received the honored central position again. The warmth of the bodies that flanked me was so intense I'd have been fine even without the protection of Van's comforter. Despite the excitement of the day and the newness of the relationships, I gave myself over easily to complete relaxation. And I slept like a baby.

We greeted the morning with another group encounter. This time we reconfigured when Michael urged me to enter his body. And I realized I had no choice but to relax enough to accept Van. What had been my greatest fear melted into intense pleasure as Van inhabited me—gently this time. I was precisely where I wanted to be at that moment and with exactly the company I craved. It was lovely.

Breakfast was also lovely. And Van was right—there was more than enough excellent smoked salmon for three. Van and Michael both were so comfortable in their skins that I too felt like a natural man. I liked the feeling. I resolved to remember it and to relive it on a daily basis. Was it that easy? It seemed so at the time. We lingered at the table for hours. I don't think one of us wanted it to end. I certainly didn't. But I also knew that people have lives. And as noon approached, I sensed that I had taken up enough of theirs.

I won't say the good-byes were tearful. But they were affectionate and heart-felt. I knew I would miss the warmth the moment I left Van's apartment. And I did. But I left with a sense of easiness that stayed with me most of the day. I didn't call Chris to tell her about my sleepover. My news would keep until Monday, surely. Perhaps I feared that talking about it would spoil the magic. I wasn't willing to risk losing the luster that adorned the memory. I kept it pure and personal as long as I could.

I phoned Van that evening to thank him again for dinner and the overnight—with breakfast! He said, "Michael just left. I'm sorry you missed him. I know he'd have wanted to speak to you."

"Van, you two are amazing. I've never felt so welcome—or so surrounded by good company as I did last night—and this morning. I'm rarely speechless, but I'm on the verge, at the moment."

"It's about you, Julian. Michael and I have been best friends for a decade, anyway. We love each other, but we haven't been lovers for a lot of years. Thank you for bringing us together again."

"I'm nowhere near the cook you are, but I'll make something soon, if you'll come to my place," I said.

"Of course," Van said. "Michael asked for your phone number. I gave it to him. I hope you don't mind."

"No, not at all," I said.

"I don't need to give you his. You'll hear from him soon, I'm sure. Be good to him, Julian. He's a precious man."

"I sensed that," I said. "And so are you, Van. Thanks again!" The conversation reinforced my feeling of calm. I realized I hadn't thought about Stuart in hours.

Chapter Seven

I told Chris about my new friends. She looked a bit stern when I told her about the 6 Train encounter, but then she said, "Oh, Michael! He's brilliant, actually. And he's a very nice man. And hot. Jules, you could do worse. And have. So? Now what?"

"I have no idea," I said. "I expect I'll see them again, but I can't say if it has any future to it. And Stuart will be back in a month. I have to concentrate on getting that right."

"I'm thinking you should concentrate first on what's best for you. You deserve some recreation, some new friendships. Don't shut down, Jules, just because you have a challenge. You're open, by nature. Keep it that way."

"You're so smart," I said. "I'm glad I have your blessing."

Michael phoned me the next day. It was great fun hearing from him. I liked his voice. I liked his sense of humor. I quite liked everything about him, really. "I was wondering if we could get together this weekend," Michael said. "Maybe dinner? On Friday or Saturday?"

I did some quick calculation and said, "Saturday sounds good. Where should we go?"

"I have a few ideas. Will you let me decide?"

"Of course," I said.

"Any food allergies?"

"Not a one."

"Good. I'll text you the details." And he did.

Michael decided on a little seafood restaurant in the East Village. He was waiting for me at the bar when I arrived. We embraced. Michael looked fabulous. And he smelled even better. I had already seen nearly every inch of his naked body, and yet I almost preferred him in skinny jeans and a nice shirt. Chris was right. He was exceptionally hot—in or out of clothes. I greeted him as warmly as I knew how.

The host seated us. "I've been here twice before. May I order for us?" Michael asked.

"Of course," I said. I was secretly relieved that Michael lifted the burden of decisions from my shoulders. I heard him order oysters and fried squid and crab sliders and a chopped salad, with a bottle of sparkling rosé to wash it all down. I was delighted. And I started to relax.

After he ordered, Michael said, "You know, Van is quite smitten with you, too."

"You're both remarkable men. I feel honored."

"Did you know Van's friends call his dick The Great White?"

"No, but I'm not surprised. Anything that monumental deserves a name," I said.

"I told Van we have a dinner date," Michael said. "He said, 'Excellent! I want to hear all about it.' Is it all right with you, Julian, if I share our evening with Van?"

"That depends on how good the food is," I said. "I wouldn't want Van to know if we're not delighted with dinner. And then there's what follows dinner. That should be delightful, too. What do you think?" I asked. I'm often reserved, but that evening I was not.

"Julian, you're a piece of work. A very handsome piece of work. Yes, I'm interested in what follows dinner, too. Will you come to my apartment?"

"Of course," I said. "A good dinner always puts me in a romantic mood. And I always kiss on the first date. After that? It depends on the kiss."

"I'll keep that in mind," Michael said.

Over fried squid—which is, of course, one of the world's great inventions—I said to Michael, "I don't really know you very well. I know you're Van's best friend. And that's a high recommendation. And Chris thinks you're stellar—also high praise. And I know that you can make love like an immortal. Hmm. Maybe that's all I need to know."

"Maybe," Michael said, "but I want you to know more. If you want it. I'll tell you anything. It's up to you."

"Of course I want to know your story, Michael," I said. "Please."

"My father is a career diplomat, assigned to New York City for much of my childhood. I happened to be born here, so I've never had to worry about passports and citizenship. And that's a good thing. Especially these days. My parents enrolled me in the U. N. School. My mother is a fine singer, but she never had the drive to pursue a career. Still, she played piano and sang, occasionally, around the house. I get my love of music from her. New York began to feel like home right away. But Madrid is home, too. I love both cities, but you notice I live here, and I only visit Spain every year or so. That should get you started. And now, *I* want to know *you*. If you'll let me."

I always hated telling my story. I almost gave Michael the lite version. I had practiced that, through the years. That's the version I had given Stuart, for instance. But then I decided Michael deserved the truth. "Growing up in Connecticut was pleasant enough, until I was seven and my mother left Dad and me."

"Jesus!" Michael said. "You must have been devasted."

"Pretty much," I said. "Dad took it hard, too, of course. It poisoned our relationship, really. I'm not saying that he blamed it on me, that his wife fell in love with another man and moved out. But I blamed him. For years. I never felt I really belonged in that family to begin with, and then . . . ? Anyway, childhood felt like a condition to endure and then escape as soon as possible. Once I got to college—at Columbia—I never looked back, except to send Christmas and birthday gifts to Dad. They're sometimes acknowledged and sometimes not."

"Thank you, Julian, for going there," Michael said. "I know it wasn't easy."

"When I know you better, I'll confess my past loves. But not tonight, Michael. Tonight is for good food and good company. Tonight is only for pleasure."

"Julian, are you playing with me?" Michael asked. "Because I like to play as much as the next guy. If you just want that, then fine. I can be a playmate. But it's not what I really want."

"Damn!" I said. "You do get right to the point!" I was quiet for a bit, trying to decide on an honest response. "I don't know what I want, Michael. Will you give me some time to figure it out?"

"Of course," Michael said. "Take all the time you need. No pressure."

"Good. The most serious question facing us now is, 'What should we have for dessert?' "

"Something light," Michael said. "Sorbet?"

"Perfect." And that's what we ordered—a little oval scoop each of two flavors: kiwi and lemon raspberry. It was the perfect ending to a delicious meal. And then we went to Michael's apartment on the West Side, in what used to be called Hell's Kitchen (still is, I guess). I decided immediately that it was a wonderful apartment—loftlike and spacious. Michael welcomed me so sweetly. I felt as if I had special access to his space, to his life.

Michael's apartment contained big, inviting furniture; gorgeous carpets with deep red as the dominant color; signed photos and other memorabilia on the walls; a collection of beautiful art glass; a few stunning paintings—eighteenth- and nineteenth-century copies of Spanish old masters, by the look of them. And at the far end stood Michael's bed. It was big, with heavy, carved dark wood and a deep-red coverlet. It looked nearly as inviting as my bed.

Michael offered me a brandy, which I accepted, of course. "This is delicious," I said. "What is it?"

"It's made by Gonzalez Byass, the sherry house that's famous for Tio Pepe. The biggest customer for this brandy is the Vatican.

"They do like nice things," I observed.

"Indeed they do," Michael said. "And so do I." There was a slight inference in his reply—a suggestion that he was including me in the category of nice things. I blushed slightly. "This has been a delightful evening."

"Yes," I said.

"There's only one way to make it even better."

"And what might that be, Good Sir?"

"If you come to my bed," Michael said as he offered me his hand. I took it, of course, and obediently followed Michael to his bed, which was even more impressive up close than I had imagined from a distance. Michael kissed me, and we began to undress each other. I resisted the urge to hurry through the process. I knew it was all good. And I wanted to savor each step. When we got to totally bare flesh, Michael pulled down the top layers of bedding to reveal many plump pillows and cream-colored sheets that were amazingly smooth to the touch—obviously high thread count. I quickly completed my survey of the bed and proceeded to focus on its owner.

Michael drew me close to him. I had nearly forgotten the softness of his lips, the sweetness of his breath, the openness of his desire, and the playful way his tongue darted through my mouth. We had never been alone, together. With Van as part of the mix we shared a wonderful romp. But this was entirely different. This was just the two of us. I was so stunned by my reactions to Michael—physical and emotional—that I didn't know quite how to behave. So mostly I let Michael take charge. I followed his lead. Eagerly. I accepted whatever he wanted of me.

Michael wanted to know my body, or so it seemed. He took a tour, really. He found something to like in every region. I simply accepted each of his discoveries. Whether he was adoring my right foot or my left ball or an armpit or a nipple, it was all good. When Michael started to get really serious about my ass, I was nearly disappointed: I worried that we were headed to the last act, and I was not ready for the climax. But the journey had been such a delight so far that I was not about to question his choices.

When Michael signaled that he wanted to top me, I spread my legs as far apart as they had ever gone, I think. He took charge and presented his dick. "Yes," I said. "Yes, Michael, I want you." He entered my body all in one seamless motion, and I accepted him totally. I also gasped and closed my eyes. Briefly. I didn't want to miss anything, so I was soon watching Michael's face again as he choreographed the dance. I loved his face while he was inside me and possessing my body. He was angelic and devilish at the same time. He seemed to glow with some inner fire. Even if it meant immolation, I'd have accepted it, if that was the price of our union.

And Michael was also mine, really. He was *my* possession just as surely as *I* was *his*, in those minutes when we were locked together. I didn't want it to end. But sex—and life—don't work that way, of course. I knew that Michael was getting close, because of his breathing and because his kisses became more fervent. I was getting close, too. He was pushing all my orgasm buttons. When Michael shouted, "*Madre de Diós!*" I erupted too. I grabbed him as firmly as I dared and accepted his gift with complete devotion. Adoration, really.

I don't remember which one of us started to laugh first, once we were mere mortals again. Michael said, "Julian, that was incredible."

"Tell me," I said. "I noticed it, too."

"Will you stay over tonight?" Michael asked. "I'd love to sleep beside you. I love having you in my bed. Am I coming on too strong?"

I laughed and said, "Yes, and no."

"Does that mean you'll sleep over?"

"Of course," I said. "Nothing would bring me more pleasure. You've already seen me first thing in the morning. If you can stomach that, then I'm all yours."

"I think I would welcome the sight of you *every* morning, but let's start with tomorrow. I have coffee, and I can fry some eggs for us. We won't starve."

"Thank you, Michael," I said. "for everything."

"Don't be silly, *mi Julianito*. Will you kiss me?"

"As often as you like," I said. "You're a great kisser. And that's important to me, actually. I'm just saying."

"Come here, you," Michael said. I fell into his arms, of course. I'm not stupid. One of the most attractive men I'd ever met had just fucked me royally—in a good way—and then invited me to sleep over in his regal bed. I luxuriated in the possibilities for simple pleasures. I wanted the ease and warmth of that overnight. I got it. Michael was a perfect bedmate. I usually sleep on the right side of the bed, but that was Michael's. So I took the left. He pulled my body to his, so that we touched at all points, and he wrapped his strong arm around my shoulder. His breath on my neck was reassuring. I felt safe. I felt complete, really. I slept.

The morning was easy. Michael was sweet and solicitous. I decided I liked him even better in the morning than at night. Everything about him. Michael in an old robe that was carelessly fastened, so that his handsome hooded dick peeked out below the sash—that alone was worth the price of admission. Michael seemed to embrace the morning like a gift. I loved his attitude and his amity. I wanted what he had.

Michael made coffee for us And, as promised, he fried eggs for us, plus slices of bread. In olive oil. It became my new favorite breakfast. We were neither of us in any hurry. "My first fitting is at 1:00," Michael said. So I'm free until nearly noon. Will you stay for a while, Julian?"

"Yes," I said. "You may have trouble getting rid of me."

"Good," he said. "That was my plan. And will you come back to bed?"

"Yes," I said. "That was *my* plan." Making love to Michael in morning light was a luscious experience. I had always assumed his eyes were brown. In fact, they were golden. I took an interest in the fine modeling of his ears. I knew the left lobe sported a gold ring. I discovered the ring was closed with a black opal bead of remarkable red and blue and green fire. I began to really appreciate the strength and beauty of Michael's hands. I took the time to explore his mouth in depth. Michael welcomed me at every turn.

"You're making it difficult for me," I said.

"How so?" he asked

"I have to leave soon, and I don't want to go."

"I don't want you to go." Michael said. "But I hope you'll come back."

"Yes," I said. "As often as I'm invited."

"So formal! You have a standing invitation, Julian. I hope you'll use it." I promised I would. I headed home with a sense of lightness and ease. But I wondered if I really deserved it. I told my brain to shut up and let me have an easy experience. Did my brain listen?

Chapter Eight

The six weeks that Stuart was away didn't exactly speed by. It was more like a crawl. There were a few welcome diversions—mostly Van and Michael—but much of it was dreary. If I hadn't had dinner with Chris once a week or so, it might have seemed unreal. But Chris kept me grounded, just as she always had. I missed Stuart terribly, of course, but I also dreaded seeing him again. I dreaded the prospect of falling for him all over again when I was supposed to be ending our relationship. Wasn't I? Surely it had no future. Did it?

Stuart phoned me from Kennedy as soon as his plane touched down. "Can we have dinner tonight?" he asked. "I have so much to tell you!"

"Of course," I said. What else could I say? "Come here, and we'll go someplace in the neighborhood. About 7:00?"

"Perfect!" I began to stew as soon as I signed off our call. But I had work to do, so I willed myself to do it and put the rest on the back burner. It worked. When Stuart arrived at my apartment, I was ready for him. Or so I thought. He rushed in and grabbed me. His kiss was passionate. I returned it in kind. How could I not? "Jules, I missed you so much! Can we make love?"

"Whoa, cowboy," I said. "You just walked in the door. I require a proper hello before you sweep me off my feet." It was just as I feared. I was falling head-over-heels all over again.

"Sorry, Jules. You're right. You're always right, actually. I didn't mean to rush you. It's just that I've wanted you so much, these last weeks. Have you thought about me?" Stuart asked.

I didn't answer his foolish question with words. Instead I embraced him tenderly and kissed him as warmly as I knew how. He responded sweetly. "Stuart, let's get a bite to eat. I haven't had anything since a late breakfast, and I'm famished. My bed isn't going anywhere. Can you wait?"

"I'll do anything for you, Jules. You only have to tell me what you want. Let's eat something."

"Good idea," I said. "How about Thai?"

"Perfect," Stuart said. And we headed out to the restaurant. We ordered the usual things in New York Thai restaurants—the soup with the chiles and lime leaves, and pad thai with shrimp. Like that. It was good. It was spicy. It was such fun to be with Stuart and to share his exuberance. I asked about his trip. "It went well," he said. "It went exceptionally well, actually. I have some reviews. How's your German?"

"Terrible."

"Not to worry. I have translations," he said, and he produced a few for me to read. They were glowing notices, the sort we'd write for ourselves, given the chance. Critics lauded the discovery of a "thrilling young tenor" with "sweetness of tone" and "flawless technique." I commented on the one that praised his "expressive use of his voice in the service of the music and the emotions in it."

"That's because of you, Jules," he said. "I didn't feel those emotions before I met you." I was floored. All my resolve crumbled. All my best instincts were bested. Did I take Stuart home with me after dinner and welcome him into my bed? Of course. But first we stopped off at the deli for some breakfast things. This was going to be an overnighter for sure. We both wanted it desperately. Perhaps at that moment, while we were buying eggs and bread, I realized we had picked up our relationship exactly where we left it six weeks before. Which was most emphatically *not* where we were supposed to be.

When we got back to the apartment, Stuart said, "I promised you my heart. I hope you believed me. I hope you'll accept this token." He handed me a little box—beautifully wrapped, as only Europeans can do it. I opened it. And there was a puffy gold heart on a delicate chain. "Will you wear it?" he asked.

"I think I've been wearing it for the last six weeks," I said. "But if you want me to wear the token as well, then, yes. It will be my honor." He walked behind me and fastened the chain. And immediately the little gold heart settled into the perfect position on my chest. We went to my bed, and then everything about Stuart that I adored was back in my arms: the feel of his skin, the *taste* of his skin, the beauty of his limbs, the warmth of his kiss, the magic of his eyes and his face and his neck and his hair and his perfect ass—not to mention the hardness of his dick and the exquisite modeling of his balls. He gave me all of that, plus his love and his sweet nature. I was overwhelmed. I had no choice but to revel in the bounty Stuart offered me. I sampled everything. I went back for more of my favorites. It was a banquet fit for gods, and there I was—a mere mortal. I did my best to deserve it.

When our passion was spent, Stuart rested his head on my chest and embraced me lightly. I could smell his hair. There must have been some lemon in the shampoo he used that afternoon. That lemon essence combined with Stuart's natural scent produced a fragrance so heady that I started to weep softly. Moments of complete joy are, after all, relatively rare. I savored it. No matter what else happened—*with* us or *to* us—I would always have that moment of perfect happiness. It might have to be enough. It *would* have to be enough, wouldn't it?

I had wanted to talk about plans for the day and the coming weeks, over breakfast preparations. It was difficult for me to concentrate on anything but Stuart. There he was—again—at my kitchen counter with sleep-tousled hair and a glorious smile. I made coffee. I served it, and then I kissed Stuart. He reached for me and kissed me back. I had to break away to get on with the business of toasting and scrambling.

Stuart said, "I love your dimples." Since he was looking at my backside, I knew which cheeks he was referencing.

"They're yours," I said. "I'll have them bronzed if you like."

"No, I want them just the way they are."

"Even better. What else do you want?" I asked. It was a bit intense for so early in the day. If I had been facing Stuart I probably wouldn't have asked that question. But I did ask it, and then I had to finish what I was doing and serve the eggs and toast. Stuart waited until I completed my tasks.

He looked directly into my eyes and said, "Jules, I've had some time to think about what I want, while I've been away. I still want you, with all my heart. I still want us. But I don't know how that would work. I know that I'll be in town for the next week, and I want to see you every possible minute. And the following week I go to Evanston. I haven't been there in more than six months."

"I understand that you have family ties there," I said. "But what about commitment? How will you resolve that? It's none of my business, but I know a little bit about relationships that are left unresolved. They fester, Stuart."

He was quiet for a bit, and then Stuart said, "Amy deserves honesty. I'm going to tell her I can't marry her. I'm going to tell her I've met someone . . . "

"Oh, no!" I said. "You'll do nothing of the sort on my account!" I flew into a rage, really. I nearly shouted as I said, "This is your situation, Stuart. I will not take responsibility for it! If you love her, marry her. If you don't, don't. But leave me out of that equation. I'm sure she doesn't want to be your back-up plan any more than I do. Man up, Stuart. Deal with it. And if you decide you still want me, then come back here and tell me why."

The breakfast table grew quiet, of course. Stuart looked ashen. "Eat something," I said. "Before it gets cold." That was advice for me as well as for him. We both took some polite bites and then pushed our plates aside. I broke the silence: "Stuart, please forgive me. I have no right to try to interfere with your life that way. It's just that I care so deeply for you, and I hate to see you trying to sit on a fence that can only split you in half. I like the whole you. I don't want you in pieces."

"Jules, you're absolutely right, as always. I thought I had been doing some growing up, but I guess I was trying to skip that part. I'm going to get it right. I hope you'll be proud of me."

"As long as you're proud of yourself, that's all that matters," I said. "Now, let me copy the reviews you showed me. I want Chris to read them. Her German is good. Let me have the originals, too." He gave them to me, of course, and I copied them all on my multi-function printer in my office. "You know, Chris quite likes you. We should get together with her. I'm sure she'd like to see you again. But then you must have a million things to do. Think about it," I suggested."

"Of course," Stuart said. "Please say hello for me. You know, some colleagues were telling me what a wonderful singer she is. I'd love to hear her some time."

"I'll bet I can arrange that," I said. "Stick with me, kid. You never know what might happen." I regretted those words before they were even out of my mouth. Stuart reached for me.

"I intend to stick around," he said. What might have been music to my ears under other circumstances instead struck a discordant note. This was surely not where we were supposed to be heading.

I knew it wasn't wise, but I said, "Stuart, I'm trying really hard to be sensible, but fuck it! I just want you in my bed. Will you join me? Will you spend the rest of the day with me? I'll do anything you ask if you agree to stay with me now, today. I'll be practical later, if you want. But now—I just want you."

"Yes, Jules. I want the same. The last time we were together there was so much going on. But to-day? I have no plans. Let's see if we can figure out something to do together."

We did find things to do that day. We made love for hours—gently, tenderly, unhurriedly. Around noontime I phoned the new food shop around the corner and ordered some salads with grilled chicken and interesting greens. Everything seemed to have avocados. They're fine with me. I had to slip on a robe to receive the delivery, but after that it was right back to naked. We ate our lunch in bed, accompa-nied by a glass of chardonnay. It was surprisingly good food, or was it Stuart? I couldn't be certain.

After our meal we banished the lunch things to the kitchen and got right back into bed. I felt fortified for the next round of lovemaking. Stuart seemed reenergized, too. We romped and laughed and kissed and fucked. And then we took a short nap. I was unwilling to lose consciousness for long. I wondered when—if ever—I'd have Stuart in my bed again. I wanted to savor every possible moment.

I loved getting to know Stuart better—his body and his spirit. I loved discovering which caresses made him shiver with delight and which tickled him cruelly. I learned what made Stuart laugh and what made him close his eyes and slip into a realm of pure pleasure. I explored every inch of him, with special attention to my new favorite regions. I decided his ass would always be my favorite, unless of course it was his mouth. I could have been content to kiss Stuart's mouth for hours, but then I'd also have been content to rim him for hours.

But then I'd be missing out on his armpits, for instance: Stuart's armpits were marvels of design, and the best-smelling parts of his body for certain. I ran my tongue wherever it could go, savoring the skin and the little thatch of hair equally. I was a happy man. I'd have taken up residency had it been possible. Stuart gave me everything he had to give. He never hesitated, not even when I wanted to do something he'd never considered before. When I wanted to suck his toes, he let me see how many I could get into my mouth at once. That made Stuart laugh, but he stopped laughing when I explored all the curves of his feet with my tongue.

Stuart was hardly a passive participant. He went on a journey of discovery, too. I gave him everything. I let him taste and handle all of me. His hands are so strong and warm that I literally felt my body was in safe hands. I could be wrong, but I always felt that same-sex couples have the easier time of satisfying their partners, simply because they have the same equipment to reference. Stuart touched me in ways that he probably would never have considered except that he realized how those touches would feel when applied to his own body. It was lovely to experience.

At one point, Stuart took an interest in the dimples he had admired at breakfast. He worked his way down. He hesitated for a moment—as if deciding if he was ready for such things—and then he took the plunge, between my legs. He was tentative at first, but he warmed to the experience and began to explore me eagerly with his tongue. I loved it. He stayed there for a long while. We were—after all—in no hurry. When he came up for air he asked me, "Jules, would you let me . . ."

"Take whatever you want. It's yours," I said.

"Thank you," Stuart said. He carefully arranged himself on top of me, and then he lifted my head and kissed me. He was still kissing me when he presented his beautiful, rock-hard dick. I accepted it immediately. He was in. I was awash in pleasure. Stuart seemed uncertain how he wanted to proceed, now that he had accessed my interior. I wasn't worried. I knew he'd figure out what he wanted. And I knew he would use me with care and respect. And that's exactly what he did. He established a comfortable rhythm with his thrusts, and then he stayed with it all the way to the end. I could tell by his breathing that he was getting close, but he resisted the urge to speed up. He gripped me tightly and let out a joyous whoop as he transferred his deepest essence from his body to mine. I accepted it with reverence. I knew he had given me himself, and I cherished the gift.

When our breathing returned to normal, Stuart started to laugh and said, "I've never done that before. Jules, thank you. That was amazing."

"No, thank *you*. *You* were amazing, Stuart. I can't even make a crack about 'practice makes perfect.' You were perfect. How did you figure that out?"

"I just thought, *What would Jules do?* And I acted accordingly. Jules, I love you."

"Come here, Stuart. I want to kiss you for a while, if you don't mind." He didn't mind, and that's what we did, for the next half-hour or so. Late in the afternoon we got up and took a shower together. I had almost as much fun lathering and scrubbing Stuart as I did fucking him. We laughed and rough-housed, as boys do. The drying off took far longer than usual because I couldn't resist the urge to kiss Stuart—often and deeply. Eventually we finished in the bathroom and I found a robe for Stuart to wear. I donned mine, and we went to sit at the kitchen counter. "Well, young man, how would you like to spend the evening?"

"The same way we spent the afternoon would be good." Stuart said.

"Smart man," I said. "But perhaps we should add a variation. Do you want to go out for dinner?" I asked.

"No, not really," Stuart said. "Couldn't we stay in?"

"Of course," I said. "We'll have dinner come to us. Are you hungry?

"Maybe in an hour or so. What do you think?"

"I think that sounds perfect. Italian?"

"Yes, please." And that's what we did. It was a wonderful day.   All wrong, but still wonderful. Couldn't I maybe find a way to make it right?

Chapter Nine

Stuart had a busy week, of course. Interviews, auditions, voice lessons, and all the other things that follow an absence from the city. I only got to see him twice, and just for dinner, really. We tried to savor our time together, but it didn't feel like much. I wasn't surprised, but I wasn't very happy, either. I also knew that I was getting a taste of what life with Stuart would be. And it didn't feel very satisfying.

Chris stepped in to buoy me. As always. I gave her Stuart's reviews. "Very, very impressive," she said. "He's obviously got it. And he seems to be focused on using it properly. That's thrilling—for him and for his audiences. For you?"

"Not so much," I said. "He's going to Evanston next week. He told me he's going to ditch the fiancée. When he told me he was going to tell her he met someone, I started shouting at him. I refused to take responsibility for his choices. It scared him, I think. I know it scared me."

"That you have a temper and a sense of outrage?" Chris asked. "It don't scare me none. I expect that in people I love. It's time he learned the same. So, what's next?"

"Well, he'll be away for a week, and I challenged him to make a clean break with his past and then come back and tell me exactly why he still wants me.

He'll probably do it. He's that kind of man, Chris. He's quite remarkable."

"But what does he have to offer you, besides his heart? What's in it for you?"

"Next to nothing," I said. "I want it all, Chris. I want a husband who'll live with me and have dinner with me every night and then hold me while we fall asleep after watching a late movie on NETFLIX. I have a life and a career. I 'm not about to consider flying all over the world just so I can have a few minutes of Stuart's time before he goes on stage. I couldn't do it. I'd end up hating him for it. And I can't bear the thought of that. And it wouldn't be fair to him, either. He needs to fall in love with a nice guy his age who wants to be his manager. They could go off on every fucking international adventure together and have a glorious time of it. But I can't do it, Chris. I just can't."

I started to cry. Chris held me. She let me blubber for a bit, and then she said, "Jules, I'm glad you know what you want and what you don't want. That's the first step. You'll figure out what to do. I have every confidence in you."

"I'm glad someone does," I said. "You've had enough of me for one day. I'm going home. Thanks, friend." Chris wished me a warm good-night, and I headed to my apartment. It was welcoming, as always. I put the events of recent days out of my mind—as much as possible—and got on with the business of getting some sleep.

Stuart phoned me when he returned from Illinois, of course. But he only had time for a quick greeting and a promise of another call soon. I was not surprised. I was sad, yes, but hardly more. A few days later Stuart called one morning to say, "Jules, will you meet me for lunch in a little while? Here on the West Side? It'll give us more time together."

"Of course," I said. I threw on some clothes and headed out. We met at a little after-theater place I hadn't seen in years. Of course it was open for lunch, too. I just never thought of it that way. Stuart looked tired but energized. He greeted me with a generous hug and a warm kiss.

"I'm so glad you could come, Jules. I've missed you terribly. I just have so much work to do. My head is buzzing. But I had to see you. And I had to talk to you. I told Amy I'm gay. I never said a word about you. I told her I've always known it, but that it didn't seem important to me—until now. I was as honest as I knew how to be. She was hurt and angry, but not shocked, I think. I doubt she'll ever speak to me again, but who knows?

"I also came out to my parents. No shock there, either, but it was time to clear the air. They were as warm and accepting about it as they could manage. They're concerned for my future and my happiness— for my safety. I assured them they might better worry about whether I can sing all nine high Cs in *Ah, mes amis.* They were great about it, really. Mom has always known, I think. Dad too, really, but he wanted to look forward to my wedding and grand- kids. I told him to expect several—grandchildren— one way or another."

Was I moved to make a little sense of my relation- ship with my own parent? Maybe. Dad and I had been so distant for so many years. Could we find a way to heal the divide my mother's exit caused? Did I even want to go there? Maybe. Would I do anything about it? Maybe. Stuart said, "Jules, you haven't said a word!"

"Stuart, you've said most of what needs to be said, I think. You don't need my approval, of course, but I *am* proud of you. Welcome to the real world, Stuart. You're going to love it. And hate it, too, of course. Let's have some lunch. They used to have a decent burger here, as I remember." We ordered. I *was* proud of Stuart, of course. I was also *deeply* sad at the inevitability of it all. I went through the motions of sharing lunch with a dear friend. When we had eaten and I had started in on my second glass of wine, I said to Stuart, "There was more."

"What?"

"There was a second part to my challenge, Stuart."

He got it, of course. He grew quiet and fiddled with his coffee cup for a moment. And then Stuart focused those beautiful eyes of his directly on me and said, "Jules, loving you has been the best part of my life. If I could spend every moment with you—waking or sleeping—I'd do it. But I can't. There's so much happening. I can't offer you what you deserve."

"Stuart, thank you for your honesty. I've known for . . . some time that we don't have a future, you and I." There, I said it out loud, too. Did I start to cry? Only very little. Stuart looked on the verge of tears, too. "That doesn't change the tenderness of my feelings for you. It just means that our friendship will have to be mostly long-distance. Should I keep your heart?"

"Always," Stuart said.

"I'll only keep it until you need it back," I said. "You'll tell me, and I'll surrender it. You'll know when the time is right." The dull ache in the middle of my chest began to spread all over my body. My limbs felt heavy and useless. I willed them to function. I rose and embraced Stuart. And then I headed home. Surely I had longed for the resolution our luncheon provided. And yet the sadness of it felt overwhelming. I decided to focus on other things. There was my work, of course. And I had a date with Michael in a few days. Everything was just as it should be. Wasn't it?

Michael phoned me often. Nearly every day. I loved talking to him. I loved the sound of his voice. It was soothing and arousing both at the same time. We had regular dates in late May, while Stuart was away and after his return and his new set of commitments. Michael and I went to trendy little ethnic restaurants in Queens or Brooklyn. We usually ended up at his apartment. I was always happy when Michael invited me to his bed. I melted into his arms and gave him my complete attention.

I gave Michael whatever he wanted of my body, and I took whatever he gave me of his. When he wanted to top me, I accepted him fully. Face up? Face down? It didn't matter. I took him inside me as easily as if we really lovers—as if we were sharing a precious bond. And when he wanted me to take charge and present him with some lovemaking of my devising, then I dived in and celebrated his body. I worshiped his handsome dick. I rimmed him until my lips were numb. I fucked him until I erupted as deeply inside him as I possibly could. And it was always exactly where I wanted to be. Every time.

But, really, what was the point? Michael wanted more than I did. I had known that from the beginning, I suppose. He wanted a love affair. I wanted a friendship that included exceptionally hot sex. I knew what was happening, but I simply refused to do anything about it. My heart was unavailable. After Stuart and I had ended our affair, shouldn't my heart have been free to focus more on Michael? It seemed logical—and desirable. But I had no idea how to go about it.

Chris phoned me one Monday morning. I was at my desk adding some frightening touches to a monster who hides under a little boy's bed. I had no trouble imagining the creature. I simply worked from memory. "Jules, you're not going to believe this, but it's true. I told you about *COSÌ* in Prague in July. Well, I just heard that the tenor dropped out. The producer is a nice guy I've known for years. I told him I know a fine young tenor who might be available on short notice. Jules, who is Stuart's agent?"

"So, let me see, now—there's you, Rebecca, Ben, and now Stuart? So, who'll sing Despina, my cousin Marie?"

"I hadn't thought of her," Chris said. "Do you think we can get her?"

"Chris, this is crazy."

"No, it isn't. It's a perfect opportunity for Stuart to sing for a large audience that's demanding but very generous. It's a perfect reason for him to learn a new role. It's a concert: He can use the score if he needs to. It's the perfect way for him to gain experience but with training wheels. I want to sing with Stuart. I hope he can do it."

"So do I, Chris, of course," I said. "I want him to have every chance to shine. I'll find out what you need to know."

"I still think you should come," Chris said. "Especially if Stuart can do it. There's something else I haven't told you."

"You want me to do the makeup?"

"That's an excellent idea, but no, it's not what I was thinking," Chris said. "We're doing three performances of *COSÌ* over a week's time, and then, two nights later, there's a concert evening of arias by various composers, with a number of guest singers. Rebecca and I will sing the flower duet from *LAKMÉ*, and Ben is going to sing—with the tenor, whoever he may be—the men's duet from *PEARL FISHERS*. It would be a great opportunity for Stuart. And I think you need to hear him. And Ben. Becca and I figure in this too, you know."

"You play rough," I said. "I'll think about it."

"If you flew in for the final performance of *COSÌ*, then you'd have a day and a half to explore Prague before the concert evening. And then you could fly home the next morning," Chris said.

"What would I do in Prague?" I asked.

"I don't know, Julian, but Czech boys are very pretty. I'll bet you'd think of something."

"Well, let me go so I can get you the agent's name. And I'll think about making the trip. It's a good thing I love you," I said.

"Ditto," Chris said. I texted Stuart. He got right back to me with his agent's contact info. I forwarded it to Chris. I had played my part. I went back to work. I also stewed and fretted about the possibility of making the trip. As I softened on the idea, I realized I would have to stay under the radar. Neither Stuart nor Ben would pick me out of a large audience in the festival theater. I would hear them—twice—and then fly home. It was doable. Lunch with Chris and Becca after the *COSÌ* would be nice. Other than that, I would be anonymous. I was unwilling to do it any other way.

I started shopping online for airfares. There aren't that many direct flights to Prague. The best deal was a package with a stop in Brussels. The layover was sensible—enough time to allow for the lateness of the first flight, but not several hours of hanging out in an airport. And then I said to myself, "This is crazy. Stuart isn't even booked for the concerts. There'll be plenty of time for travel plans after it's official." I let go and got back to my projects.

Chapter Ten

It took me a while to work up the courage, but I did invite Van and Michael for dinner. I figured that while I was at it, I might as well invite the girls. Finding a date that suited Chris, Rebecca, Van, and Michael was not easy. But we found one—a Thursday in mid-June—and we locked it in. I knew I could never match Van's kitchen prowess—nor Chris's, for that matter—but I knew I could offer hospitality. My living room is comfortable, and I have a nice dining table as well. I chose the apartment because I liked the openness of it, and because I felt it could easily become Party Central. And yet I'd never thrown anything you could really call a party in it. Most of my celebrations had been of the one-on-one variety. That was about to change.

I can create a menu; I can choose wines that are festive but not too important; I can welcome guests and make them feel special; I can put food on a platter or a plate and make it look inviting. In other words, I can host. Cooking is a separate skill. I may not possess that gene, but I learned to compensate for it years ago. I considered hiring a handsome young man to help me. That was too stupid. I could handle it. Couldn't I?

It was nearly summer, so I decided on a lot of cold food: I would blanket my table with *charcuterie* and relishes, Middle Eastern salads, Russian pickled things, and cool *tapas*. Like that. I could buy all of it. No matter what followed, there would be enough food for a complete meal. I decided we should have soup next—chicken broth, maybe. *Real* broth. I had a source for that. And maybe some little *tortellini* in it. Yes. And then a cool roast, or something. With a green salad. The girls offered to bring dessert. And I'd get some fruit and cheese. Yes, it would work.

There was a lot to organize. I spent a few days gathering things—tasty things. I visualized the presentation, and then I let go of the results. I knew I had plenty of glassware, silverware, and plates. I owned far too many napkins, and some of them were even ironed. I was in a bit of a tizzy when everyone began to arrive that June evening, but it was nothing I couldn't handle. Van gifted me with a small plate decorated with a sketch by Raoul Dufy. I knew they existed, but I had never actually held one. It looked like the essence of summer. Michael brought a huge bouquet of white peonies. I had the perfect vase for them—a low one for the middle of the dining table. Chris and Becca arrived, together, with a Mozart torte—appropriate, after all.

All my friends know how to pour themselves a glass of wine. Very few introductions were needed: Van had never met the girls. We fixed that. Michael and Becca discovered they had worked together at a Met event. And then we were all old friends. It flowed. I almost relaxed. The table looked festive, I must say. We sat and began to sample the goodies. It was an unhurried process, and I got to spend most of dinner with my guests. Michael's peonies were not only lovely, but they began to open during dinner into the most exquisitely sensual blooms—like Michael himself; like the friendships around the table.

When everyone was sated, we adjourned to the living room for coffee and post-prandials. Michael tended bar. We relaxed and complained of being overfed. It was a successful evening. I knew it would be, but then things can always go wrong, can't they? We escaped mishap. We drew in the family circle. We were safe.

It was a weeknight, after all. Around 10:00 Van said, "I have to be up before six tomorrow, so I can make it to court on time. I'm going to head home. Julian, what fun! Many thanks." At the door, he embraced me and said, quietly, "Jules, I hope you know how important you are to Michael. And to me, for that matter. I'll call you soon." And he was gone.

The girls also claimed early morning commitments. As Chris was leaving, she kissed me and said, "You make a really beautiful grownup, I must say."

"Ditto," I said.

Rebecca had a warm kiss for me as well. She whispered in my ear, "I've seen your bed. I want to see more of it."

"I know you say that to all the boys, Becca," I said. "But let's talk. Try to stay out of trouble." And then it was just Michael and me. I turned to him and said, "Please tell me you don't have to leave now, too."

"No," he said. "As a matter of fact, I was hoping for an invitation. I was hoping you'd ask me to stay over."

"I'm so relieved," I said. "I was afraid I'd have to *compel* you to stay. Which I'd have done. Please come here." And he did. "I have such a good time with you, Michael. Could we do this more often?"

"Julian, I'd be happy to talk about a *forever* arrangement. But I can tell when you're playing with me. Just so you know, I'm serious. I want you. If I can't have all of you, then I'll settle for what I can have. But I want you, Jules. I won't pressure you. I'll wait."

"Jesus, Michael!" I said. "You're like a hero in a romance novel. You're entirely too good to be true. And yet you're in my arms. Will you kiss me?" He did, of course, and then I said, "Look, let me organize a few things, and then we can turn in."

"I'll help," Michael said. "I'll clear the table. Why don't you load the dishwasher? Everyone has his own method." Michael brought plates in and quickly slipped leftovers into ziplocks. I rinsed and loaded. Michael said, "We could talk, you know. You once promised to tell me about your loves and losses."

"So I did," I said. Do you think this is the time? Over dirty dishes?" Michael looked patient, as he so often seemed to be with me. I opened up. "I fell in love when I was twenty. No, that's not the whole truth. I fell in love with Christina when I was eighteen. And that love has never wavered. But when I met Benjamin—two years later—I knew almost instantly that he was the man for me, that I wanted to bind my life to his, that he was my North Star." I grew quiet. Michael waited. I opened up again: "If Ben had fallen out of love with me, I'd have figured out a way to get over him. I think. But he didn't fall out of love with me. I think. He simply needed to follow his career path to London and God knows where else in Europe. And he built a career. But it's not here. I've only seen Ben twice since he left New

York, after our graduation. Could you bring in those wine glasses? We're making great progress. Michael, could I take a breather? I don't think I have any more of that in me tonight."

Michael embraced me. "Thank you," he said, "for telling me about you."

"And now it's your turn," I said.

"Very well," Michael said. He brought in the last of the glassware. I filled one half of the sink with hot, soapy water and the other side with warm, clear water. I dipped and dipped and drained. I handed Michael a lint-free linen dish towel. He began to dry the glasses. And he began to speak: "I dated a bunch of different guys, from about age seventeen. I guess I was a pretty wild kid. It was fun. It was exciting. My parents disapproved, so that made it even better. I didn't really focus on one man until I was maybe twenty-five. When I met Charley, then everything changed, and I wanted to spend all my time with him.

"We took an apartment together. I got my first job at the Met. Charley worked on Wall Street. We invented a routine. It was like a real life for the first time for me. I loved it. Charley loved me. He was happy. It was all good. And then one day Charley had—an episode of some sort. It terrified both of us, of course. I got him to a doctor, who diagnosed epilepsy—adult onset. There were meds. It looked manageable. But then one day while Charley was at work he had a massive seizure and stopped breathing. Nobody—not even the paramedics—could revive him.

I quickly dried my hands, reached for Michael, and wrapped my arms around him. "I mostly cried the first year," he said. "Then I ran out of tears, and

Bruce K Beck

I haven't cried since. I met Van a year later. The sex was great—in the beginning—but the friendship was even better. And it still is."

"Thank you, Michael," I said. "I think I'm beginning to know you. And that's a good thing. Please come to the bedroom." And he did. We undressed. When I turned down the coverlet I wondered why it had taken me all those weeks to invite Michael into my bed. I loved having him there. It felt perfect—Michael beside me in the center of my universe. We held each other.

"Great bed," Michael said.

"All the greater for having you in it," I said.

"Julian, I love you," Michael said. I had no response, so instead I tightened my embrace. We held each other. We kissed, and eventually we slipped into sleep. Mine was deep and dreamless.

Stuart got the gig in Prague. Somehow, I knew he would. He was on a roll. His schedule was heavy already, and then he had the added responsibility of learning a new role—and the beautiful Bizet duet as well. I knew that Stuart would rise to the occasion. I sensed that he would be just as at-home with the classical purity of Mozart as he would be with the romantic lyricism of Bizet. And I guessed Stuart would be just as comfortable with Italian as with French. It was a lot of work. It would consume all of his time. I already knew that I would not be seeing him, so our separation was no longer an issue—more or less.

At first, the forced time apart made me unhappy. But before long I realized that it was a blessing. It was a chance for me to get on with my life—a life that did not include Stuart. He phoned me one evening in late June and said, "Jules, may I come over? I need to see you."

"Of course." What else could I say? I threw on a robe and waited. Stuart arrived in about a half hour looking ghostly pale and agitated. I said, "Come here. Let me hold you." Stuart fell into my embrace and started to cry. I couldn't remember that I had ever seen real tears fall from those beautiful green eyes of his. I merely held him and waited. I had no idea what was happening, but I didn't need to know more than that he needed me. It was enough information. When Stuart calmed down a bit, I led him toward the kitchen and sat him down. I also poured two tall cognacs.

"Thank you, Jules," Stuart said. "I feel like such an idiot."

"Why, because you had a human moment? We all have them, you know."

"No, because I'm terrified, Julian," Stuart said. "I'm swimming in deep waters, and I don't know if I can stay afloat. Mozart and Bizet next month, and I'm singing Bellini and Donizetti in the fall. I don't know if I can do it."

"Is that all?" I asked. And then I started to laugh. And then Stuart began to laugh, too. "Welcome to showbiz," I said. "You'll find a name for that terror. And you'll learn to kick it to the curb whenever it threatens to take you over. You'll never lose it, I expect. I *hope* you'll never lose it. It's part of who you are—and your talent." We were quiet for a bit.

Stuart began to look more like himself. "Do you want something to eat?" I asked.

"Well, maybe a scrambled egg."

"Why not?" I asked. "I'll join you." I scrambled a few eggs and toasted some slices of challah I found in the freezer. It was almost like our mornings together. Almost. Except that this meal had no promise of a future in it. We ate. We finished our cognac. And then I said, "You obviously need rest. Come to bed. There's nothing you have to learn that can't wait until morning." Stuart followed me to the bedroom like an obedient child. We undressed and got into my bed. I pulled up the comforter. I held him. Stuart clung to me as if I were his only anchor. I knew that feeling only too well.

Did I make love to Stuart, that June night when he returned to my bed—probably for the last time? Absolutely not. I couldn't have done it—to him or to me. He was just as precious as he had been the first time he lay beside me and the last time we made love. My dick was just as hard as it was every time Stuart was near me. But the world had changed big time since May. And I had changed with it. Was I maybe even learning a little bit about responsibility?

_________ *Chapter Eleven*

Prague, of all places. I'd never been there. I had a sense of Budapest and Vienna, even Berlin. But Prague? I knew Mozart had debuted some works there. I had heard about a house, in the suburbs, where Mozart and Costanza lived while he was writing, what? I had heard that the food—other than pastries—was pretty bad. But that was right after the liberation. A friend told me about a hotel in the former secret police headquarters where you could pay extra to stay in Václav Havel's former cell. No matter what glowing reports I heard of the new Czech cuisine, I was still skeptical.

But really, none of that mattered. I was going to Prague as a music lover, not to mention the lover—or *former* lover, to be exact—of half the cast of the concerts I'd be hearing. Chris booked a room for me at a hotel not too far from the theater and not too expensive. I would be fine. And it would only be a few nights, after all. I own a few suits. I choose not to wear them under ordinary circumstances, not even to attend the Met. This trip was not ordinary. I got out a dark suit—surely one navy suit would be enough for both concerts—and white shirts and ties. Play clothes for in between. I prepared. I packed. And then I flew.

The audience seemed delighted to be there in Festival Hall, that lovely summer evening. They also seemed delighted with the prospect of hearing Mozart. Is *COSÌ FAN TUTTE* a frothy opera? I always thought it's equally fraught. It lacks the darkness of *DON GIOVANNI*, of course. That one always felt like a date-rape story, to me—with beautiful music, of course. But with *COSÌ*, I think the various tests and deceptions could be heartbreaking, except for the music. I'm not particularly interested in some of the recent productions with languid and foolish lovers who slip and slide into various configurations. I don't think that's what Mozart wrote. I think every note is about the human condition. That's what I hear. And that's certainly what I heard that July evening at Festival Hall in Prague.

The overture always sends me into a weepy zone. Then the ruses and deceptions are quickly established, and then comes *Soave sia il vento*, the little terzetta early in Act I, where the sisters and the crafty old man pray for gentle winds to bless the voyage of the boys—on their fictitious naval campaign. It's the first Mozart I ever heard—or at least the first I was aware of. I sang a choral version of it when I was a choir boy. It is burned on my brain. The sweetness of *Soave sia il vento* goes so much deeper than musical comedy. But never mind me.

Chris was radiant. Dame Kiri was my first Fiordiligi. Chris was even better. Her *Come scoglio* in Act I was fierce, as it should be, I think. No froth there. And her *Per pietà* in Act II had the perfect sadness of lessons learned. Not the autumnal quality of the Countess in *FIGARO*, but a bit of maturity. And Rebecca's Dorabella was equally fine, showing her usual blend of power and sweetness. The mezzo gets a bit less attention, but Becca was never one to surrender focus. They're both so smart about what they do. I'm always amazed when I hear them.

Ben's Guglielmo was, well, Ben. I knew he sang Mozart beautifully. I heard him sing arias from *FIGARO* back when we were together. No surprises. Ben was handsome, confident, creamy, perfectly musical. Ben was just what he had always been—a wet dream with a voice. Only maybe better than ever. Did I yearn for him? You betcha.

How can I describe Stuart's Ferrando? He took not one modern interpolation. His rendition was as pure as the driven snow. When Stuart sang *Un'aura amorosa*, late in Act I, the audience tried, many of us, to wait respectfully for the last bars of music. And then we all went apeshit. Stuart seemed visibly shaken by the roar in the hall. He was gracious. He was humble. But the applause and calls of "*Bravo!*" showed no signs of abating. And then came calls of "*Encore!*" Eventually Stuart looked to the conductor, who nodded and signaled his orchestra to go back to the beginning of the aria. It was only the opening arpeggio that silenced the audience. In fact, the orchestra played it three times before there was quiet in the house. And then Stuart sang *Un'aura amorosa* again. The second time, he sang it maybe even more sweetly than before.

It was as thrilling a moment as I've ever spent in the theater. It was one for the history books—at least for my own personal journal. It was also the very moment when I knew—without the slightest equivocation—that I had most certainly lost Stuart forever. He belonged to his audiences. He was no longer mine, no matter how sweetly Stuart remembered me and felt true love for me. As if I needed the confirmation, that concert taught me that our affair was fucking over.

The rest of the performance was delightful. The rest of the cast—the Despina and the Don Alfonso— were local favorites who charmed the audience at every turn. They charmed me, too. As did the orchestra. When the performance was over, it was all I could do to refrain from going backstage to congratulate the cast. But it was Stuart's night, not mine. I couldn't intrude on it. And I couldn't bear the thought of seeing Ben in his dressing room, like the old days. I couldn't do it. I went back to the hotel and had a drink in the bar.

At a café the next day, I stood as the ladies arrived. I applauded and called, *"Brava! Brava! Bravissima!* I wasn't the only patron who had attended the concert—the night before or perhaps one of the other two performances. There was polite applause throughout the room. Chris and Becca were gracious. "Julian, don't ever do that to me again," Chris said as she kissed me.

"Yes, dear," I said. "I must say, you two make Schwarzkopf and Ludwig sound like amateurs."

A gorgeous young man with creamy skin and long eyelashes appeared at our table. "Forgive me, ladies, but would you sign my program? My name is

Gregor, but my friends call me Greg." he said. The girls signed his program, of course.

As Becca was writing an inscription, Chris said to me, *sotto voce,* "What did I tell you about Czech boys?"

I stood and offered Greg my hand, which he shook warmly. "Julian," I said. Greg smiled very sweetly. And then I said, "This is my first visit to Prague. If you have the time, I could use some help learning about the city."

"Of course," Greg said. "It's a lovely city. It would be my pleasure to show it to you."

"Excellent," I said. "Could we start after lunch?"

"Perfect."

"Will you join us" I asked, indicating the vacant chair at our table.

"Thank you, but I'm with my friends, just over there," Greg said. "I'll watch for you, so we can leave the café together."

"Thanks so much, Greg," I said. We ordered some lunch and a glass of wine. "How about that Stuart last night?" I asked.

"I knew he could do it," Chris said.

Becca said, "Stuart is so professional, and a pleasure to work with. And he's so cute! I think I'm in love."

"Get in line, dear," Chris said. "You have all of Prague as your rivals.

The waiter brought us our choices. Everything looked very simple and fresh. And it smelled wonderful. Later, over excellent pastry, I said, "The concert last night was exceptional. I had such a good time. Isn't it remarkable? I've screwed the best singers we know and I'm still living alone."

Rebecca said, "Whoa, wait a minute. I've never had the pleasure."

"Quite right. We could fix that," I said.

"What do you think, Chris? Is he worth it?" Becca asked.

"Jules is the most considerate lover I've ever known. I'd be happy to give him a toss right after lunch. But watch your heart, Rebecca. He can't be trusted with hearts."

"I guess I deserved that. It still sounds harsh, though," I said.

"Sorry, dear," Chris said. "Compared to other men, I suppose you have a rather good record. But speaking of broken hearts, your next one is standing just over there." She indicated Greg, who was waiting for me at the bar. "Have a lovely day, Jules. Call me next week." I assured her I would. I kissed the girls good-bye and headed to the bar to join my very pretty tour guide. He smiled easily, and we headed for the street.

It was a perfect European summer day—lots of sunlight and big, puffy clouds, with a comfortable temperature that made sightseeing a treat. Greg started my tour at St. Vitus Cathedral, of course. And then on to Prague Castle. Like so many other European capitals, Prague is a great pedestrian city, with eye candy at every turn—architectural and human. It has gems from gothic to Art Nouveau to modern. We went to the top of the Petrin Tower (even taller than the Eiffel Tower, I learned). The view was stunning. We crossed the Vltava on the Charles Bridge, of course—the one with all the statues of saints—and we explored the east side of the river.

Greg showed me all the usual tourist sights, plus some of his favorite places a bit off the beaten path.

I especially liked seeing the Jan Hus Memorial in Old Town Square. New Yorkers all know the Jan Hus church on the Upper East Side—a bastion of progressive values for generations, and a sometime host to great antique shows in the basement. I happened to buy my bed there, but never mind that. It's always good to see the roots of our familiar institutions. Greg and I stopped for a coffee about 4:00. It was excellent. "Your English is perfect," I said. "How did you manage that?"

"Everybody studies it these days," he said. "I like English. My friends and I speak it most of the time when we're together. I still speak Czech with my parents, but that's about it. My French is good. I can get by in German and Italian. What languages do you speak?"

"You've got me there. I'm a typical American," I said. "I can still read a little French, from school, and I'm interested in music, so I can fake a little Italian when I have to. Oh, and I live in New York City, so I have at least some whorehouse Spanish. That's about it."

"You're funny," Greg said. "And handsome. But you know that."

"I'm not so sure. But I know you're a delight to look at, and to be with. Will you have dinner with me tonight, Greg? You're the only friend I've made in Prague, and I hate dining alone."

"Sure," Greg said. "I'd like that. No one should be alone on such a beautiful evening. I have an idea. There's a restaurant with a view. And you should see the building it's in, anyway. We could finish our tour there and then go upstairs for dinner. Does that sound good?"

"Perfect," I said. "Lead on!" And that's what we did. We saw Wenceslas Square and the Powder Tower, eventually wending our way to Dancing House. I had never heard of that office complex co-designed by architect Frank Gehry. Fred and Ginger is the local nickname. I found that maybe more charming than the actual structure, but it was undeniably impressive. And the view from the top is even more so. Greg had called ahead, so there was a table waiting for us.

The menu was inviting. Obviously, things culinary had progressed nicely since the days that friends told me about when dinner in the Czech Republic meant choosing which kind of pig, which kind of cabbage, and which flavor bread dumpling. No, this was a different experience, luckily. Instead we were able to choose a lovely river-fish soup, veal braised in beer with mushrooms and ethereal little potato dumplings stuffed with cranberries, and a refreshing salad. It was all delicious.

Something chocolate for dessert is always fun. The torte was exceptional in a region where excellent desserts are the norm. Over very good coffee, I told Greg, "It certainly is a beautiful evening. I'm not certain I could find my way back to the hotel. Will you guide me?"

"It would be my pleasure. We can walk, if you like."

"Yes please. I'm in no hurry," I said.

"Neither am I. I have an early class tomorrow, but no plans for tonight."

"In that case, why don't you come up to my room?" I said. "I have a bottle of brandy, so we could have a nightcap there."

"Perfect," Greg said. "I love brandy."

"Good," I said. We headed toward my hotel. He said it was about a thirty-minute stroll. I put my arm casually on Greg's shoulder. He smiled at me. We came to a section of sidewalk that was quiet and rather dark. Greg stopped, turned, and kissed me. It was a very warm kiss. "I want more of that," I said.

"So do I," he said. We walked the rest of the way in silence. We reached my hotel and headed up to my room. Even in the greenish light in the elevator Greg was stunning to behold. I ushered him in and poured two brandies, as promised. And then we got down to the business of more of those kisses. Greg seemed as interested as I was—always a pleasure. I knew nothing about Greg, really, except that he was an exceptionally beautiful Czech college student with a warm smile and a sweet nature. Perhaps that was all I needed to know.

We undressed each other and got into bed. Greg's creamy skin continued on and on, all the way to his toes. I took a particular interest in his dick, which was quite ample. You never know. He also took a strong interest in *my* dick. That's always nice, but it's not my favorite thing to do in bed. I let Greg hang out there for a while, and then I pulled him up for another of his kisses. And then I asked, "Will you roll over and let me explore the other side of you?"

Greg smiled and assumed the position. I started with his shoulders and the nape of his neck and worked my way down his strong, lean spine. When I got to the base of it, I realized Greg had a remarkable ass. Perhaps not as perfect as Stuart's, but close. I spread Greg's legs and dove in. He responded warmly. My tongue could only go so far. I wanted more entry—more depth. I moved into position to top him. Greg urged me on with his body language.

I presented my dick—carefully, respectfully. I waited. I kissed him. Greg said, "*kurva mě.*"

I don't understand a word of Czech, but I got it. I entered. Slowly. He received me. I savored the handsome young body beneath me. I warmed to the sweetness of Greg's spirit as well. I tried my best to honor him—to honor the intimate intersection of our two bodies. And when I couldn't delay it any longer, I simply gave Greg the best that was within me. He accepted my offering.

Greg had an offering for *me,* as well. We rolled him over and I encouraged him to come on my face. It was warm, and generous, and delicious. It was delightful. We came down from our high. I lifted my face from Greg's belly long enough to ask, "Are you certain you won't sleep over tonight?"

"Thanks, Julian, but I really can't. I have an 8:00 class, and I can't go there looking like I just did what I just did with a handsome American. But I'm really glad I did it. I feel like I just made love to a man for the first time."

"Ouch! First times always make me feel a little nervous," I said.

I don't mean that I've never . . . done that before. I just mean that it felt like making love for the first time."

"That's very sweet," I said. "And so are you. I don't suppose I'll see you again."

"Are you going to the last Festival concert tomorrow night?"

"Yes, I am," I said.

"We could meet in the lobby before," Greg said.

"Perfect," I said. And I sent Greg on his way home.

Before the concert, Greg said, "The baritone from two nights ago is singing again, I think. He's so handsome. What's his name?"

"Benjamin Hickock," I said.

"I wouldn't mind being his boyfriend."

"Well, good luck," I said. "I doubt he's available. But if you can get him, I guarantee it would be worth the effort."

"You know him?"

"From another life," I said.

"You seem to know everyone," Greg said.

"No, only the best of them," I said.

"I believe you, Julian."

"What do you think of the tenor, Stuart Kreisler?" I asked.

"Vocally, he's amazing. And he's so cute. I'd love to meet him."

"Maybe I can help," I said. "Go backstage after the concert and ask for the soprano, Christina Grimaldi. She'll remember you from the café. I'll text her and ask her to introduce you to the boys. That should do it." I sent the text.

"Wow, thanks, Julian. This has been such fun. Will I see you again?"

"Well, that's difficult to say. I don't get to Prague very often. Like, never. What about you?"

"Actually, I'm planning a trip to New York in late August, before the fall term starts. May I call you?"

"Please do," I said. "I'd be more than happy to see you again, Greg. I think you're delightful. And it's not just because you're so pretty. I think you're a very sweet man, and I want to thank you for making my visit to Prague such a pleasure." The concert was quite good. The orchestra was exciting, and most of the singers were excellent. My friends were never better. The girls sang the shit out of the Flower Duet, and the boys were quite wonderful with the Bizet. Stuart was so worried about it. But he sailed through it with ease, as if he'd been singing it all his life.

The chemistry between Stuart and Ben was remarkable to experience. I totally believed they were best friends. It was quite moving—for the rest of the audience, too, I expect. It was another triumph for all four of them. At the end of the concert, I said goodnight to Greg and reminded him to ask for Chris backstage. He kissed me very sweetly, and we parted. I headed back to the hotel and got ready for bed. And in the morning I flew home. It was a good trip. It was a necessary trip. Did I maybe learn a little something, too?

Chapter Twelve

"Welcome home!" Michael said on the phone. "How was your trip?

"It was just fine, Michael. Good music, good food, good drink. No complaints. Did you miss me?"

"I always miss you when I'm not with you," Michael said. "May I show you how much?"

"I hoped you would," I said. "My place or yours?"

"My place, I think," Michael said. "Come over, and I'll figure out something for our dinner."

"Give me time to shower. I'm feeling sticky from the trip," I said.

"No, come over. We'll shower together."

"Smart man," I said. "I'd like that. I'm not always very good company when I'm jet-lagged, but I'll give it a try."

"Good," Michael said. "Just get over here and let me pamper you." I did as I was told. I didn't even unpack. I just brushed my teeth and headed for the West Side. Michael welcomed me with a warm embrace.

"Remind me to go away more often," I said.

"You'd better not," Michael said. "I want you close by. Now, how about that shower?"

We stripped and put our clothes on the bed. "Lead the way," I said. Michael ushered me into his bathroom. I'd been there before, of course, but never for a shower. The room was generous and inviting—like its owner. I especially admired the bidet. So civilized. So sensible. So un-American. Michael had installed a big tiled area at one end of the room with shower heads and a drain. It was merely an extension of the floor, and yet it was obviously graded so that water flowed in the right direction. We kissed. We walked to the shower. Michael adjusted the water temperature. When he decided it was perfect, he welcomed me into the spray.

"I have to pee," I said.

"Go ahead," Michael said, as he knelt before me. I was reluctant, but I did as I was told. I let loose, and Michael accepted my offering on his face, on his chest, in his open mouth. He stood and kissed me while he still retained a little of me in his mouth. I thought I might hate the taste of it. I did not. The fact that he had blended the two of us into that kiss may have softened the experience. I wasn't sure. Would I try that again? I wasn't sure. Except, of course, if Michael wanted it. Then I would most likely do—anything.

Michael scrubbed us all over with a huge natural sponge. And when he was certain the back wall was sufficiently warmed by the shower spray, he pressed the front of my body against the tiles and then entered me from behind—gently, carefully, masterfully. I accepted Michael instantly. I was in a state of perfect pleasure, spread eagle against the wet, warm tiles with an extraordinary man behind me, filling me with his body and his spirit.

"I want to see you in my clothes," Michael said, when we had finished our shower and dried off.

"But Michael, you're so much more built than I am. Nothing would fit."

"You have a great ass, Julian. I'll bet my jeans fit you fine. And a shirt's a shirt. Get dressed. We need to have a welcome-home dinner. Take these socks. You don't really need shorts, do you?" I did as I was told. I slipped into Michael's jeans and they did fit me, of course. A bit differently from the way they fit him, but well enough. So well, in fact, that I was aroused by the concept of inhabiting Michael's space. It was all I could do to focus on other things long enough to lose my wood. Michael laughed at me. Easily and warmly. I laughed, too. Michael handed me a shirt—white, with blue stripes. "Is this WASPy enough for your taste?" I put on his shirt. And we were ready to go out.

"There's a little Brazilian restaurant a block away. A *feijoada* is just what a voyager needs. And a *caipirinha* is just what the doctor ordered." We took a table and decided on the usual, wonderful Brazilian specialties. It doesn't get much better than that: black beans with lots of cured meat served with sliced oranges and pickled onions and stir-fried shredded collards. Heavenly. But I'll skip the *farofa*—I think you have to be born to that. Manioc meal has the texture of sawdust, in my experience. Even when It's washed down with a Brazilian daiquiri (more or less, but don't quote me on any of this to your Brazilian friends).

"What is it between Spain and Portugal?" I asked during dinner.

"You mean why neither believes the other exists— or deserves to exist?" Michael asked.

"More or less," I said. "It does look that way."

"If I had the answer to that dilemma, I'd be a candidate for the Peace Prize. It's old, old political animosity. It's probably about the unification of

Spain and the fact that Portugal never fell in line to accept Madrid's rule, the way the other provinces did. More or less. And Portugal had lots of money from their New World colony—thank you, Brazil, for this lovely food. So Portugal enjoyed considerable support from Rome, too. And we've all seen what happens when politics and religion mix. Do we really want to talk about all that over this delicious dinner?" Michael asked.

"Sure," I said. "A little controversy stimulates the appetite."

"Have you been to Brazil?" Michael asked.

"Once, during Carnival," I answered. "I liked it very much."

"And Portugal?" Michael asked.

"No, but I once heard a pirated copy of the Lisbon *TRAVIATA*. Does that count."

"Almost," Michael said. "I'll take you to Lisbon some time, if you like. It's a beautiful city. But I never learned Portuguese, so we'll have to brush up on our French before we go. There's no Spanish allowed." Michael and I talked and laughed easily through dinner. It was a perfect restorative for a weary traveler. As we headed back to Michael's apartment, he said. "Julian, please stay over tonight. I've missed you so much. I want you in my bed. I won't bother you. I won't keep you up late. I just need to have you beside me."

"Thank you for the invitation, Michael. How could I say no? As someone in a Cole Porter song says, 'My will is strong but my won't is weak.' Of course I'll stay."

"Good," Michael said. "I have an early morning, so we'll both be up and out at a reasonable hour. Unless you want to sleep in, Jules. You're welcome to do that. *Yo soy un idiota*—I've never given you a key. I'll fix that as soon as we get back. You already have the key to my heart. Why shouldn't you have the key to my apartment as well?"

I stopped right there, on the sidewalk, and embraced Michael. I was experiencing a big surge of strong feelings—gratitude, lust, exhaustion, and something that was quite like love, and yet *not* love. Or so it seemed at the time. We made our way back to Michael's. "Let's get you to bed," he said. And that's what we did: I slipped out of Michael's clothes—reluctantly. I brushed my teeth, and that was about it. We got into bed, and Michael pulled up the comforter. He held me so gently and whispered, *"Duerme bien, mi amor precioso."* I felt perfectly warm and safe. I slept.

In the morning, Michael was up long before I was, showering and making coffee. It was the coffee aroma that woke me, I think. Michael brought me a cup. *"Buenos días, mi Bello Durmiente,"* he said. And he kissed me—morning mouth and all. I kissed him back. "I hate to disturb you, Jules, but I have to show you how the door lock works." He also showed me that he had put out some bread and cheese and Iberian ham for my breakfast.

"Michael, you're entirely too much," I said.

"I was hoping for just right," he said.

"And you achieved it," I said. "My mistake."

"I left a robe for you on the bed. Please enjoy the morning, and please stay as long as you like. Will you call me later?"

"Of course," I said. "Have a terrific day." And Michael was off to work. I put on his robe and took my coffee with me to the kitchen. I sat quietly for a while, enjoying my delicious breakfast. And then I neatened up Michael's bed, dressed in my clothes, and headed out into the real world. My apartment was waiting for me, just as I had left it. And my work was waiting for me on my desk. I unpacked from my trip and got to work. It was a productive afternoon. I felt calmer than I had felt in weeks. Surely it had much to do with Michael. Didn't it?

Chapter Thirteen

Stuart's career took off like wildfire. Many of his bookings were a year or two in the future, but they were commitments, for certain. And word-of-mouth in the industry fanned the flames of stardom. Stuart would text me to tell me about an upcoming *LUCIA* at Covent Garden, or *BOHEME* at La Scala, or *TOSCA* in Houston. One milestone that really caught my eye—my ear, really—was Stuart's announcement that he would sing *LA FILLE DU REGIMENT*—nine high Cs and all—in San Francisco. I decided I would probably have to show up for that one.

One evening I said to Chris, "You know, the Met should create a new production of *I PURITANI* for you and Stuart. And a new *SONNAMBULA.*"

"Why don't you talk to Mr. Gelb about that?"

"Good thinking," I said. I'll get right on it."

Chris said, "I see Ben now and then, you know. He always asks about you. I always tell him he should call you if he wants to know how you are."

"Thanks, dear," I said, "but that ship has sailed. Let's try to live in the real world."

"Good thinking," she said. "Why don't you take me to dinner? Is that real enough for you?"

"Quite," I said. And that's what we did.

❧

Stuart phoned and asked me to have dinner with him. I accepted. We met at a Daniel Boulud restaurant across from Lincoln Center—the sit-down-dinner one. A little dressy, I thought, but not overly expensive. Stuart looked great. He greeted me warmly. Over main courses Stuart asked me, "Why didn't you tell me you were going to Prague? Why didn't you come backstage after the concerts?"

"Stuart, it just didn't make sense for me to be there, and yet I had to hear you. And Ben. And the girls, of course. Chris encouraged me to make the trip. But I couldn't intrude on your success. It was yours, not mine. And you were quite wonderful, you know. Your *Un'aura* was the finest I've ever heard. And the Bizet? What you and Ben did with it was flawless. And it had nothing to do with me."

"I disagree, but I think I understand," Stuart said. "I have something awkward to tell you: It was totally unexpected, but I need to ask you for my heart back."

"Who's the lucky person?" I asked.

"You know him. It's Greg, from Prague."

"Stuart, that's perfect! He's a great guy. And so good looking. If it were up to me to choose a mate for you, I couldn't have done it better. Congratulations, my friend!" And in that moment I silently returned Stuart's heart in mint condition. Did Stuart know that I had actually taken a hand in their meeting? I suppose so. More or less. I didn't bring it up, and neither did he. But I was secretly proud of my backstage machinations. And Stuart seemed wildly happy with the outcome.

I wasn't wearing the gold heart Stuart gave me. I hadn't worn it in weeks, because I doubted my right to it. I didn't mention it. I figured there would be a time and place. "Greg's coming to New York next week," Stuart said. "He wants to see you. Can we plan something?"

"Of course," I said. What else could I say? I had no intention of getting together with Stuart and Greg, but then, perhaps I could be persuaded. My attempt at matchmaking worked, and that was a good thing. But spending an evening with Stuart and his new beloved felt like more than my old heart could process. I left the restaurant feeling a great mixture of joy and sadness. So, what else was new?

When Stuart texted me with a time for our meeting with Greg, I accepted. I also texted Michael and asked him to join us. He agreed, to my great pleasure. I thought Michael would enjoy meeting both Stuart and Greg, but I also liked the idea of having a date of my own instead of being just the odd man out. Was it selfish? Probably. But it was also practical.

It was Greg's first night in town, so Stuart wanted him to have an iconic New York experience. He decided on the Oyster Bar at Grand Central Station. I hadn't been there in ages, but I had watched the other eateries and the food hall grow in vibrancy in recent years. I thought it a terrific idea. Michael was also pleased with the choice.

The four of us met by the clock in the middle of the Great Hall. Greg gazed up at the (backwards) constellations on the ceiling for the first time. We showed him some of the other architectural features of the building, including the grand corridor with the corners where you can stand against the arch and your voice will carry across the vaulting to the opposite corner, as if it were amplified. Now there are acoustics even the Met might envy.

The host at the Oyster Bar showed us to our table. I was so glad Michael had agreed to join us. What might have seemed an awkward evening instead felt nothing but pleasant. We ordered wine and lots of oysters in various forms. I took Greg to the counter to watch the counterman prepare a pan roast in one of the gleaming old steam kettles. The process remains a treat to watch, I always thought. Greg seemed to enjoy it, too.

"It's good to see you again, Greg," I said. "We promised to meet in New York, and here we are."

Greg kissed my cheek and said, "Thank you, Julian. My new life is all because of you. I love Stuart so much, and I would never have met him if you hadn't stepped in to arrange it."

"I'm really glad for both of you. Promise you'll be very good to him."

"Promise," Greg said.

I handed Greg a tiny box. "This is Stuart's heart. It's yours now." Greg took it, of course. "We should get back to the table before they eat all our oysters," I said. And that's what we did. Michael and Stuart were deep in conversation when we returned.

"Stuart and I have just been comparing notes," Michael said. I blushed deeply. "We agree that you're a quality guy."

"Thanks for the vote of confidence," I said. How stupid was it for me to agree to have dinner with

three present or former lovers? I got over the embar-
rassment of it all quite quickly. The oysters were
great, both the raw and the cooked. It seemed the
perfect first dinner for Greg in New York City. The
four of us had a delightful evening. The first of
many? Perhaps. Or just a momentary blip on life's
radar screen? Who could say?

Chapter Fourteen

Michael phoned me the first Friday in September. "*Perdóname, querido.* I can't get away for the weekend after all. We're behind on prep for the new productions. We have to make two hundred fifty pieces for the new *RING CYCLE* alone." We had planned to go to Tanglewood for the last concerts of the season. "But I'm going to take off Sunday evening no matter what. How do you feel about Spanish music?"

"When I was a kid, I loved the Andrés Segovia concerts on PBS. That's about all I can tell you. What did you have in mind?"

"There isn't that much Spanish music in New York, but there is a concert on Sunday evening. It's at the Recital Hall at Carnegie. They do it every year. It's sponsored by *Amigos de la Zarzuela.* Do you know about zarzuela?

"I thought it was a dish."

"That's just a play on words. Zarzuela is a sort of popular opera that combines song and dance. It's operetta, I guess. Very Spanish. And It takes legit voices to pull it off. A lot of the music is very complex. You might like it. It's fun."

"If *you* like it, Michael, then I'm sure I will, too. Let's go, if you think we can get tickets at the last minute like this."

"I know the producer, actually. And he always has a few seats put aside for emergencies—like this one. I'll call him right now if you want to go."

"Let's do it," I said. I'd have agreed to go to a dog-fight if Michael had asked me. But instead, he invited me to attend a performance of a popular entertainment I knew nothing about. I was delighted.

I met Michael at the Recital Hall about 7:00. He picked up our tickets at the box office, and we went next door to the bar at the Russian Tea Room for a glass of wine. Michael tried to prepare me for the experience to come. "Like opera," he said, "zarzuela is about sung plays that audiences know and love. It tends to have more dance than opera does. Other than that, it's quite similar. Montserrat Caballé used to sing a favorite zarzuela aria as an encore at the end of her concerts. And there's a famous duet—I can't remember the name of it—that she and José Carreras used to sing when they appeared together. I'm sure you can find all that stuff on YouTube if you're interested.

"Tonight we'll hear some arias from various plays, and there will probably be at least two dance groups as well. And some classical guitar, most likely. It's all very Spanish, but I think you'll find that it's noth-ing like Flamenco, except maybe for the guitar work, I suppose. That may sound a bit like what you've heard before. But the arias? Another art form en-tirely. I'll be interested in your reaction to it all."

"I'm sure I'll love it," I said. And I did. Michael was spot-on with his descriptions of the work. I was surprised I had spent so many years devoted to music without encountering even a snippet of the zarzuela arias. I can't imagine it as a steady diet—only Mozart would do that for me—but as an occasional snack? Absolutely. And experiencing it with Michael was a factor in my pleasure, of course.

Michael invited me to his apartment after the concert. I was happy to accept. It was a beautiful evening, so we walked—ten blocks south and a few blocks west. We were there in less than twenty minutes. Michael let us in and poured us a brandy. We sat on a sofa—quite close together—and enjoyed the proximity and the elixir. I marveled at the sweetness of Michael's nature. I had never known him to do or say anything petty—anything unkind.

"What fun, Michael! I'm so glad you suggested that concert," I said. "I wouldn't have missed it for anything."

"Oh, good," Michael said. "I've always liked Spanish music, but never more than tonight—with you." I put my head on Michael's shoulder, and he embraced me gently. "*Te quiero, mi Julianito,*" he said. I'm not stupid. I got it. I just didn't have words to respond. So instead I snuggled in a little closer and savored the warmth of the moment.

"Julian, tell me about your mother," Michael said.

"Jesus, Michael! You certainly know how to change the subject."

"I'm not pushing you, but I'd like to know about her. I think it's important."

"Of course, Michael," I said. "You're right, as always." I had the official version of my memories. It was well rehearsed. But I decided Michael deserved as deep a dive as I could manage: "I adored her when I was a little child. She was so pretty, and so full of life and fun. She read to me every night, tucked me in, and sang to me—strange lullabies, really: folk songs, or Frank Sinatra hits, or songs that Nina Simone recorded. Then I started school, and I was never certain what I'd find when I got home in the afternoon. Some days Mom was just as she had always been, and some days she was sitting at the kitchen table with a bottle of wine and a faraway look in her eyes.

"I had no idea what was going on. And she couldn't—or wouldn't—tell me. Our bedtime ritual ended. Dinners with Dad were increasingly tense. I was on edge, and my schoolwork began to suffer. I started to 'act up' in class, which just wasn't like me. I was sure it was all my fault, of course. That's what kids do. So I decided to become a model child. I tried to fix things. And we all know how effective that is. Instead, the tension between my parents increased. And then one night, Mom came to my room and sat on the edge of my bed, just as she had done in the happy years. She said, "Julian, always remember that love doesn't change just because you can't see the person you love." She touched my cheek and looked at me intently, as though she was memorizing my face. She kissed my forehead. She left my room. And the next afternoon—when I got home from school—she was gone."

"Thank you, Julian," Michael said. "I don't think I can know you without knowing that child. I can't change the past any more than you can, but I want to be a part of your future. If you'll let me. I want to comfort you. I hope you'll let me love you. It's what I want most."

I looked at Michael and wondered what I had done to deserve him. Nothing surely, and yet he was in my arms. I had nothing appropriate to say, and so instead I said, "Let's go to bed." And that's what we did. Michael made love to me with his usual tenderness and care. I was in bliss. And afterward, I slept like an infant.

In the morning, while Michael made coffee, he said, "I know it's a holiday, *querido*, but I have to go to work soon. I wish we could be together today, but I can't manage it. Actually, I wish we could be together always." He paused, and then he said, "I don't know, Julian. I don't always know when you're listening to me."

I reached for him and said, "I always listen to you, Michael. I just don't always have a reply. Will you give me some time?"

"Of course," he said. "Take all the time you need." We had a bite of bread and cheese, and then Michael had to leave. I threw on my clothes and headed out with him. He smiled as warmly as ever, and yet I sensed a new sadness behind his eyes. Or had I only imagined it? I walked Michael to the subway station. We kissed and promised to speak later, in the evening. He disappeared into the station. I walked uptown for a while and then caught a crosstown bus. They were running on a holiday schedule, but I didn't mind the wait. I was in no rush.

As the bus headed east, through the Park, I looked at all the familiar landscapes I had passed hundreds of times. And I wondered what the fuck I was doing—*with* and *to* Michael. I wondered what was wrong with me that I couldn't seem to give myself over entirely to the sweetness of that new re-lationship. It was comfortable, without a doubt. It was satisfying, truly. Michael was warm and kind, he was pistol-hot, and he loved me. What more could I desire? I didn't want to think about it. I knew the answer, of course. I just wasn't willing to face it. Surely Michael didn't deserve to be strung along. Surely he deserved a total commitment. And surely I couldn't find such a thing in my heart. Could I?

Chapter Fifteen

**I knew Rebecca was scheduled to sing CAR-
MEN** in late September, at Lyric in Chicago. I like
Chicago, and Lyric is a wonderful old house. When
Becca asked me to come to her opening night, I was
more than happy to do it. Michael wanted to go to
Chicago with me, but it was his busiest season, after
all. Traveling alone is not my favorite pastime, as
you know. But I can do it. I even booked a room at
the Palmer House to complete my "Old Chicago" experience. Rebecca asked me to come to her dressing
room before the performance. I bought a huge bouquet of red roses from a street vendor on my way,
and I showed up at the opera house late in the afternoon.

"Hi, handsome. Come in. What did you bring
me?" I kissed Rebecca and presented the roses.
"Ooooh, they're almost as pretty as you are. Come,
sit here."

"Becca, you look fabulous," I said.

"I guess terror agrees with me. It's just the usual
opening night jitters. I'll be fine once I'm on stage.
But I don't want to talk about me, if you can believe
it. It's Chris. She has breast cancer."

"Shit!" I said. "How bad is it?"

"Not very, I think. As these things go."

"Why didn't she tell me?" I asked.

"Oh, Julie, you know Chris. She thinks she can white-knuckle anything. I wasn't supposed to tell you, but I thought you needed to know. And now you do. Chris'll never forgive me for breaching her confidence, but . . . Thank you for coming, Baby. She'll be fine. And now, I have to be murdered in a few hours, so I need my solitude to prepare for it. I think you'll like the production. Oh, here's your ticket. We can't forget that. Come back here afterward, if you want. I'll let you take me out for a late supper, and after that . . . ?"

I went out for a glass of wine and a bite to eat. I remembered a restaurant at Union Station that was an easy walk from the theater—just a few blocks south and then across the river. I hadn't been there in years, and it was fun to go back. The walk also gave me time to process the new information about Chris. Surely Becca was right, that Chris would be fine. Wouldn't she?

Rebecca's Carmen was quite wonderful. The audience ate it up. I learned later that a Met scout was in the house and that Rebecca received an offer for two years hence. Didn't I tell you? I always knew she'd be there, sooner or later. I wondered if Stuart might be her perfect Don José. And if so, then how would I help that happen? Hmmm . . .

I did go backstage after the performance. Rebecca was caught up in a whirl of after-show excitement and attention. There were people everywhere, waiting to get close to her. She called to me and grabbed me fiercely. "Thanks for coming, Julie."

"I wouldn't have missed it for the world. And you were perfect. But I expected nothing less," I said.

"Sorry, but I can't go out with you tonight," Becca said. "My agent wants me to meet with—you know how it is. Have a safe trip home. And take good care of Chris. She needs you, more than she knows. I love you, Little Julie. Go with God." Rebecca kissed me warmly, and then I managed to squeeze out of her dressing room and out of the opera house.

I walked back to the hotel. It was windy, of course, and fall was coming on faster than back home. But I enjoyed the walk. I had a snack—and a stiff drink—in the hotel coffee shop. And then I turned in. My flight home was uneventful, mercifully. It would have all seemed perfectly pleasant had I not been faced with the prospect of health issues visited on my best friend. Unsettled, I think, is how I felt. And that was not likely to change for some time.

⌕

"Did Becca tell you? That bitch!"

"But why didn't *you* tell me, Chris? How could you keep it from me?"

"Because you have enough to worry about, Julian," Chris said. "Because this is nothing. I've never been sick a day in my life, and I don't intend to start now. They removed the lump the day before yesterday. I start radiation on Monday. I told them, 'No chemo that makes my hair fall out or that makes me retch all the time.' I have some important concerts in November, and I'm going to be 100% when I sing

115

them. You know, one of them is at Avery Fisher Hall, or whatever the fuck they call it now."

"Come here," I said. I embraced Chris firmly, and then I released her and said, "Shit! Did I hurt you?"

"See! *That's* why I didn't want you to know. Jules, go home. I'm fine. I'll call you next week, especially if the radiology technician is cute. Go!"

"You won't get rid of me that easily," I said. "Chris, come here. Let me hold you." And I did hold her, as gently as I knew how. Chris let down her wall of strength for the first time in ages. I hadn't seen her cry since the day I left her. Perhaps she hadn't. Cried. Since that day. Seventeen years before. I don't know. "You must be terrified," I said.

"Of course I'm scared. I'm not an idiot."

"I'll make you some soup," I said. "Maybe that's not the best idea. What if I move in with you for a week or so? Maybe not. I don't know, Chris. I don't know what I can do for you. You have to tell me. And 'Go home!' is not an option."

"All right, sweetie," she said. "Let's get on with our lives as normally as possible. I don't expect you to pretend that nothing's wrong, but I also don't want you to handle me with kid gloves. Why don't we have dinner?" Chris asked.

"So smart!" I said.

"I wish that omelet place were still around the corner. Anyway, the new La Goulue is quite good. Why don't we go there?" And that's what we did. It was early, and they had a table for us. I had never really had a sick friend before, so I was making up my behavior as I went along. I was too young in the 1980s to understand about all the gay men who were dropping out of sight. And then in the 90s, when I was old enough to sort of get it, the Epidemic had morphed into something so much more manageable that it was beginning to feel like the Post-AIDS Era. Of course it wasn't, but it felt that way.

I wouldn't try to write about the AIDS crisis. I'm the wrong source of information. Talk to activists. Talk to health workers who man the front lines. Talk to survivors. Talk to those who survived their dead friends and partners. I have nothing to contribute to that dialogue. But I try to listen to those who do. And when I found out about Chris's illness, I began to wonder if we're not in the grip of another epidemic. Or have women always suffered and died in such large numbers? It's puzzling—and deeply disturbing.

I've never owned much jewelry. It never interested me particularly. But I did have a large turquoise ring I had always loved. I knew that in the Southwest, the First Nations believe turquoise is healing. I had no better medicine to offer. So I gave Chris the ring and said, "Please wear this. Let it help you heal. If you like it, then keep it. If you don't like it, then return it to me when it's work is done. But wear it now." Chris understood, of course. She put the ring on her index finger and gave me a thank-you kiss.

Chapter Sixteen

Michael and I met for dinner the day after I returned from Chicago—the day after I confronted Chris with her silence about her illness. Michael said, "It's good to have you back. I don't like it when we're apart."

"Neither do I," I said. That was the truth, and yet I wondered why it seemed so easy for Michael to sail through his feelings of longing for me while I always seemed to be in a navigational fog of my own making. We were sharing an excellent porterhouse at Gallagher's. For years I had been passing the cold locker in the front window with all the aging loins of beef with their tags on them—like toe tags in the morgue. It was an iconic part of the Theater District, and yet I had never dined at Gallagher's. I was expecting gruff service and an interior that looked its age. Instead I was pleasantly surprised to find the restaurant warmly welcoming and richly comfortable.

"I was pleased to hear about Rebecca's opening-night triumph. She deserves it," Michael said. "You know, you've always thought of her as Carmen, but I think of her as Dalila. And it just occurred to me that Stuart's Samson would be a perfect complement. If he can sing Bizet, then I'm sure he can sing Saint-Saëns. We have to be careful, though. We don't want a repeat of what happened to Leyla Gencer."

"Who?" I asked.

"Leyla Gencer was a soprano with a big following among gay men. She was before our time, but I've heard some recordings. It's a big voice with an edge to it. Some thought of her as the road company Maria Callas. Anyway, the opera queens were clamoring for Gencer to appear at the Met. And according to legend, Mr. Bing was so put off by the association that he refused to hire her. Whatever the reason, she never did sing at the Met. And we don't want that to happen to Rebecca."

"No, we don't," I said. "I hadn't thought of the politics of it all. I doubt that Gelb is homophobic like that, but before I organize fan clubs for my friends, I guess I'd better be sure to encourage diversity."

"Good thinking," Michael said. "But I'm keeping *your* fan club small. I want to be the only member. Speaking of which, there's going to be a meeting of the club at my apartment in about twenty minutes. Will you attend?"

"Of course," I said. "You know I like to mingle with my fans." And that's what we did: We headed to Michael's and settled in for another warm, cozy evening together. Only the closer and more intimate we became, the more I started to feel on edge.

"I love you, *Julianito*," Michael said. I bristled. "You don't seem to like it when I tell you I love you. I do, you know."

"Well, don't," I said.

"Why not? What's wrong?" Michael asked.

"With you? Nothing," I said. "You're perfect, Michael. You're handsome; you're hot; you're smart; you're talented; you're a kind friend and a considerate lover. You're exactly what every man needs—what every gay man desires. You're the stuff that dreams are made on. It's me. I can't do this. And I don't really know why. That's not true. I know why, I just don't know what to do about it. I just know I can't give you what you need—what you deserve. It's not in me. And I won't fake it."

"Is it Ben?" Michael asked.

"In a way," I answered. "But he's only a ghost from my past. When I'm in your arms he can't intrude on us. But when I'm alone? That's different."

"Thanks for your honesty, Jules. I'll confess I feel like I've just been punched in the gut. But I'll learn to deal with it. So, what does this mean for our friendship? Will I see you? I hope so."

"As long as you know I won't change, and if you still want to see me, then sure. We're good friends, Michael, after all. But please don't make love to me. That I couldn't take. I find you irresistible. So, I need your help. Because it wouldn't be fair to you, if we made love. It wouldn't have my whole heart in it. It wouldn't be forever."

"At the risk of living a cliché, I'm wondering if you'd be willing to let me down easy, Julian. I wonder if you'd spend tonight in my bed, so I have that memory. If I promise to let you go in the morning and then never pressure you again, will you give me tonight?"

"You're good. I'd be a fool to refuse you, Michael, if you're sure it's what you want. I've wanted every moment of our time together. I wish it didn't have to end. But it does. If you want tonight, then I'll give you everything I have to give. Tonight. And I'll cherish the memory of it maybe more than you will."

Our lovemaking took on a new urgency. We had to fit eternity into one night. I responded to Michael's caresses with a new warmth. He worshiped my body with complete devotion. Michael's bed became like a furnace, and I dared not retreat from the flames. Instead, I welcomed the heat, the danger, the thrill. If it had consumed me totally, it would have been worth it. If I never made love again in my miserable life, that one act would have been enough.

In the morning, Michael and I had coffee and a bite together, just as if it were any other morning. We got ready to face the new day. We decided to head out together, as we had done before. As I was preparing to leave, I put Michael's door key on the night table. The finality of that simple act chilled me to the marrow. Was I doing the right thing?

Chapter Seventeen

Van phoned me the next week. "I'm going to have a long lunch break tomorrow. Why don't you meet me? There's a Vietnamese soup joint just below Canal Street. I think you'd like it."

"That's a great idea, Van," I said. "Of course I'll join you." I wondered how long it had been since we had seen each other. Probably not since my dinner party. I was very fond of Van, so I was excited about seeing him. But then I had recently broken up— more or less—with his best friend. So that event seemed to hold the potential for some awkward moments. I decided not to dwell on it. I got on with my life.

The next day, at noon, I was delighted to see Van. We embraced warmly. I had never seen him in "business attire." Van looked very professional. "What should I order?" I asked when we were seated.

"Most people get some variation on *pho*. I like the one with the egg. If you like tripe, then consider that. It's especially good here. But they're all delicious. I tried the tendon once. Interesting texture, but once was enough for me. You might love it. You look great, Julian. I've missed you."

"And I've missed you, Van. I was just thinking how handsome you are in a suit and tie," I said.

"It's just another kind of drag," Van said. "It's part of my work. I prefer leather." We ordered soups. I ordered a beer. Van ordered tea. We talked easily about concerts and the new opera season. Our soups arrived. Mine was delicious. I was glad I had chosen tripe, as Van suggested. The chewiness of it was a perfect contrast to the softness of the rice noodles. It was all entirely pleasant until Van asked, "Julian, what happened?"

I knew exactly what he meant, of course. I avoided Van's gaze and focused on my soup for a bit. Eventually, I had to answer. "I figured you'd ask me that, Van. And still, I don't have an answer, as much as I'd like to. All I can tell you is that my heart is not my own."

"Julian, I think you're ducking something. I wouldn't push you on this except that Michael is so precious to me. I want his happiness. I thought you were the key to it. I still do."

"Van, you're amazing," I said

"Let me tell you a little bit about Michael. When we met, he was devastated from losing Charley. He told you about Charley, I assume."

"Yes."

"Michael hoped I could fill the void. So did I. And I think our friendship has been an anchor of sorts for him through the years. But I can't give Michael what he most needs. I can't be the center of his universe. I think you can. I *know* you can. I thought you knew that. So, I'll ask you again—what happened?"

"Jesus, Van! I know you're an advocate, but I suspect you'd make a great prosecutor. I'm starting to sweat, and I don't think it's the *pho*."

Van smiled, maybe for the first time that meeting. "I'm not trying to be tough, Julian. I just need to know what's going on in the lives of two men I care deeply about. I can't force you to talk about it, but I think you know much more than you're willing to share. I thought we understood each other better than that. I thought we could say anything without fear of judgment. I thought we shared a bond. What if I remind you of your membership in the Brotherhood? Does that count for anything?"

I didn't burst into sobbing tears, right there in the Vietnamese soup parlor. But I did get misty. Van had touched all the right nerves. He forced me to go deep. I started by saying, "I'll gladly renew my vows. I'd be on my knees in a heartbeat if we weren't on your professional turf. Van, I want you to know the truth, as I know it. This is the best I can do:

"The man I fell in love with when I was twenty still holds my heart. I've tried to reclaim it, without success. I've made attempts at a workaround through the years. I've even convinced myself I was free of him. At times. But after I met Michael, I began to realize that no limitations would do. Michael deserves a totally committed heart. Anything less—anything that isn't genuine would be unspeakable." I took a deep breath and fell silent.

"Thanks for that, Julian. Perhaps I understand," Van said. "Just tell me: Do you love Michael?"

"Of course I love him, Van. How could I not? He's maybe the most lovable man on Earth." I was a little shocked at the sound of that. "It's just that I can't give him what he deserves. What I have to give is not good enough. It's incomplete. And I won't pretend there's more."

Van said, "Julian, I'm hoping you'll give this some more thought. Believe me, I don't mean to trivialize your concerns. But I want you to reconsider. I believe that what you and Michael share right at this moment

is enough. I think you can build a permanent relationship on it. But it isn't up to me, is it?"

"Van, sitting here, listening to you, I can almost believe it's that simple," I said. "But I know that when I
leave this restaurant and head home, Ben will come
right back into my head and my heart. The memory of
him is relentless. But I promise I've listened to every
word you've said. And thank you, Van, for your concern. Michael is a fortunate man to have such a friend.
And so am I."

Van and I finished our lunch, embraced, and
parted. Just after he had started south, to the courts,
Van stopped and turned. I was still standing in the
doorway of the eatery, watching him walk away from
me. Van waved. I waved back. And then I headed for
the 6 Train station. A great sense of emptiness flowed
over me. But before too long—as I had feared—Ben
filled the void. He was inescapable. And he had been
a part of my life for so many years that I barely noticed
his presence.

On my way home I asked myself, "Should I give Michael a call?"

To which I replied, "Why?"

I had an answer, of course, "Because he's a good
friend and you haven't spoken to him in a week. Not
since you kicked him in the gut."

"Leave him alone," I said to myself. "You've done
enough damage already." That angel of my nature—
whether it was a better one or not—won the argument.
I didn't phone Michael. I simply went home, returned
to my desk, and got some work done. I also cried a little
at one point. But it wasn't anything I couldn't handle.
Was it?

Chapter Eighteen

Chris's treatment did not go quite as smoothly as we had hoped. Her doctors did start her on a chemo regimen that made her feel sick all the time and that made her hair fall out. She was brave. She took the anti-nausea meds. She concentrated on wellness. The process seemed quite brutal to me, and I was only on the outside looking in. The key to Chris's resiliency—beyond her spirit—was knowing the ordeal was temporary: In a month or so she would be back to normal. More or less. By the time she was feeling better, her appearance had taken a hit. And November would be an important month for her.

I phoned Michael to tell him Chris needed his help. I felt awkward about reaching out to him, but Michael was his sweet, generous self. He said, "No problem. I have her wig form on file. I'll pull it out today and start something. Tell Chris not to worry. We'll have her looking exactly her beautiful self." And that's what he did. I was at Chris's apartment when the messenger delivered the box.

Chris approached the whole thing with trepidation. "Open the fucking box," I said. She did, of course. And she unpacked the hairpiece Michael made for her. The hair was precisely her color and texture. I could see that from a distance. She slipped it onto her head, and it instantly fell into place. A little adjustment, a little styling tweak, and she would look perfectly normal. And wasn't that the goal, after all? Chris was delighted. She phoned Michael immediately to thank him.

I phoned him as soon as I got home. "Michael, that's amazing what you did. You saved Chris's life, you know."

"Isn't that a little dramatic, Julian? I'm not a healer."

"I'm not so sure about that," I said. "But thank you for your friendship. It's precious to me."

"As yours is to me," Michael said. I was feeling in danger of having a Michael meltdown. So I ended the conversation and headed to my desk. Before I could get too deep into the project at hand, my phone rang. It was Becca. I had to pick up:

"Hi, Julie. It's your favorite mezzo," she said.

"I thought you were my favorite *singer*," I said. "But let's not play favorites. What can I do for you?"

"You can knock some sense into Chris's hard head, that's what you can do. I haven't seen her since before I left for Chicago. And she won't take my calls. I'm turning to you because you're an interested party, after all."

"I know, Becca, and I've never known Chris to hold a grudge like this. I'm not sure I know what to do," I said.

"It's just that we have concerts coming up in a few weeks. One of them's at Geffen Hall. I'm sure she told you. She's going to sing the Exultate, and we're going to sing the Barcarolle together. Now, Chris can play the diva all she wants, but we're going to sing those concerts. And I won't do it with a hatchet between us."

"I get it," I said. "Let me figure out something. I'm going to Chris's tomorrow evening, to take her to dinner. Are you free?"

"I'll cancel everything."

"Come here about 6:30," I said, "and we'll go together."

"Thanks, Julie. See you then!" I wasn't sure what magic act was needed to fix this mess. But I'd have to do something, surely. I kept that thought in the back of my brain for the next twenty-four hours.

Rebecca arrived promptly at 6:30. I poured us each a glass of wine. "This is exciting, Julie," she said. "We're never alone together like this—in an apartment with a bedroom. What a pity there isn't more time," Rebecca sighed.

"Our day will come," I said. "Meanwhile, let's head to Chris's and get this over with." We were silent on the walk to Chris's apartment building. I had nothing clever up my sleeve. I had decided to simply react to the situation. It didn't feel like much, but it seemed the best plan. I was quite nervous as I rang Chris's bell. So was Becca, I think.

When she opened the door, Chris's smile curdled when she saw Becca beside me. She'd have slammed the door on us if I hadn't stepped into the doorway just in time. "Go away," she hissed.

"Chris, we have to talk," Rebecca said.

"Traitor!" Chris screamed.

"Stop it, Chris!" I shouted. "Right now! I will not be a party to this nonsense!" Chris backed off. I had never barked at her, in all the years of our friendship.

But I did then. And she pulled right back on her heels. She froze, really, and Rebecca lunged forward and embraced her. It was awkward, but really, what could Chris do?

"Chris, you know that Julie had to know, don't you? Don't think I enjoyed breaking your confidence," Rebecca said. "I only did exactly what you'd have done if the shoe was on the other foot. You know I'm right. Chris, I love you. And you love me. I did what I had to do. And now you have to forgive me for it."

Shit! I thought. *What opera did they steal this scene from?* The ice was broken. Chris and Becca both got a little weepy. They resolved their difference. I was relieved, to say the least. And I was starting to get really hungry. "Let's get some dinner," I suggested.

"Yes, let's," Chris said. "Just give me a minute to pull myself together." She headed for her bedroom.

When Chris was out of earshot, Becca turned to me and said, "Nicely played, Little Julie. When did you become so wise?"

"Since I started hanging out with you, I guess," I said. "But let's not try that again. It will have lost the element of surprise." Chris returned, looking exactly herself. And three old friends went out for dinner. A celebratory dinner, really. It was a reaffirmation of life and love and the unbreakability of the bonds of friendship. As I headed home—alone—I wondered if I had forged any others—other bonds. Surely I had failed with most of them. Just as I had failed so miserably in my friendship with Michael. Hadn't I?

Chapter Nineteen

When my phone rang that morning, I glanced at it and considered whether I cared to pick up. The call was from Stuttgart, of all places. I answered. "Hi, it's Ben. How are you?" he asked.

"Well, thanks," I said. "And you?

"Very well. I'm calling to tell you I'll be in New York next week. Will you have dinner with me?"

"Of course," I said. What else could I say?

"Good," he said. "I'll email you the particulars when my plans are finalized. Will you make a reservation? Some place nice? I don't know anything about the City anymore, but I'm sure you do."

"I'll take care of it, Ben," I said.

"Good," he said. "I hoped you would."

"It's nice to hear from you. It's been a long time," I said.

"Yes, well, I'm looking forward to seeing you," he said.

"Yes," I said. And he hung up. I had a little Ben moment—a mixture of inflation and deflation, the same as I had experienced over the last years whenever I saw him—or thought of him. And then I got on with my day. I had work, thank God. One of the big publishing houses gave me a book to illustrate. It was a likely best seller by a top-list author. They wanted the cover art and a line drawing for each chapter. It was challenging. It was satisfying. I had a life, yes?

Ben did email me with a date for our dinner meeting. I hadn't been dwelling on it, but I did think carefully about dining options. I considered, briefly, the newish restaurant at Lincoln Center—the one with grass growing on the roof. The food is good, and the décor is interesting, but it seemed too obvious. I wanted something nice but rather public. Not too romantic. Nothing too ethnic. Nothing too trendy. Nothing in Brooklyn. Eventually I decided on Le Bernardin. I hadn't been there since—never mind how long ago I was there. But I knew it was still solid.

It was a fluttery afternoon for me, the day of our dinner date. Really—Ben, of all people. In New York. About to have dinner with me. I tried to make it a light thing. I did some work. I took my time showering and getting ready. I decided to wear a suit—which I really dislike doing. But I assumed Ben would do the same. I chose my favorite tie: It has splashes of red and blue and gray that take on an iridescence in the weave of the silk. It reminds me of a Japanese illustration. It makes me happy to look at it. I tied it. I slipped on my jacket. I checked my mirror and decided that I looked good. I headed to the restaurant.

Ben also looked good. He looked fabulous, actually. I was glad I had put on a suit and tie. It was a way of honoring the occasion, but the formality of it was also light armor against assaults on the heart. We were seated, and we ordered cocktails. I hadn't tasted a Negroni in how long? Ben smiled easily, as he always had. I noticed that the little touches of gray in his beard, on either side of his chin, made him look even handsomer than ever. I might have swooned, had I not developed—through experience—a Ben-proof heart. More or less.

When he moved his right arm, I noticed Ben was wearing the heavy Navajo silver bracelet I gave him for Christmas our first year together. It was more than I could afford, but I wanted him to have it. It suited him perfectly. He said he loved it. He said he'd wear it always. He also said he'd love me always. He said a lot of things. We both did. And there we were having dinner at Le Bernardin nearly seventeen years later, and Ben was wearing that bracelet. It still suited him perfectly. I couldn't guess the message there, if indeed there was a message.

The servers pampered us, and they offered some possibilities—off the menu—for both food and wine. We made choices. I went for something safe. I think it was something to do with striped bass. I was in no mood for adventure. I have no memory of what Ben chose. We talked. We reminisced a bit. We ate. We drank excellent wine. It was all perfectly pleasant. I began to relax—truly—and to wonder why this reunion had seemed so, well, fraught.

"Why didn't you come backstage to see me in Prague?" Ben asked.

"Several reasons, really," I said as I gathered my thoughts. "I didn't want to intrude on your success; I couldn't decide if I really needed to see you again; and the fact that I had recently ended an affair with Stuart seemed to complicate things even more."

"Stuart's a fine singer, and a fine man. I'm glad I was able to work with him."

"You two sang beautifully together. I've never heard a better pairing of male voices."

"I quite like Greg," Ben said.

"Yes, he's a sweet boy."

"You set them up, didn't you?" Ben asked.

I gulped and said, "I knew I wasn't right for Stuart, as much as I might have wanted to be. And I sensed that Greg *was* right for him. I gave Cupid a little shove, just as any friend would do."

"You're a remarkable man, Julian. But then you always were." I was feeling a bit off balance. Ben ordered Chartreuse with our coffee. I always preferred the color to the flavor, but I was happy to share the experience with him. And then he said, "I've been offered a teaching post at Juilliard."

"Ben, that's wonderful!" I said.

"I don't know exactly how they found me, but someone suggested me to the Dean of Vocal Studies. I interviewed with a talent scout in Frankfurt. And they made an offer."

"Have you decided?"

"Yes," he said. "I start in January. There's a lot to do to dismantle my existing life. But I'm excited about the new one."

"Of course you are," I said. "You'll find New York much changed, but still wonderful."

"I'm sure I will," he said.

"Where will you live?" I asked.

"They've offered a small housing stipend for the first year. I'll find something. But honestly, the only place I really want to live is with you, Julian." I think I gasped audibly. "It was always you. You know that, don't you?"

I was speechless for a bit. Ben ordered another Chartreuse. I sat. I studied the handsome man across the table from me as if he were a stranger. And then I found my voice: "So, you thought I'd wait fifteen years for you? Suddenly I'm convenient? After all this time? I think that's cruel, Ben. I'm not certain I know you anymore. I'm even wondering if I *want* to know you anymore. I need some time, Ben. As if I haven't had enough already. I don't know. Let me breathe. That announcement of yours just sucked all the oxygen out of the room. Would you mind if I just went home? Call me tomorrow, if you want to. Thank you for dinner." The hostess retrieved my coat quickly. And I was out of the restaurant and onto the street.

I walked for a while. It was a nice, still evening, and I really did need some air. That part of the West 50s is not very exciting for pedestrians, but I didn't need any more excitement. After walking for about fifteen minutes, I hailed a cab. It was one of those strangely tiny cars that look comfortable enough until the driver heads out into traffic and starts to bounce the occupants like so much freight. Was I in danger of losing a very expensive dinner? Yes. But we made the trip without my hurling in the back seat. And I had rarely felt so glad to be home.

I hung up my suit. I wasn't making a whole lot of sense of the evening, but I wasn't willing to fall apart. *Fuck!* I thought. *How could Ben do this to me? How could he try to sing his way back into my life? Isn't it enough that he's owned my heart all these years? Now he suddenly wants the rest of me, too?* I cried, just a little. And then I slept, just a little.

Ben did phone me, of course, about 9:00 in the morning. "May I come over?" he asked.

"No," I said. "I'm not up to that. Not this morning. But I'll meet you somewhere. In a couple of hours. If you like."

"Yes, please," Ben said. "Just tell me when and where."

"Okay, Ben. Why don't you meet me at Maison Kayser—the one on Third Avenue in the low 70s—at noon?"

"Of course, Julian," Ben said. "I'll see you then."

I wasn't certain what I was getting myself into. But really, what else could I do? The love of my life wanted to see me. More than that, he wanted to move in with me! I couldn't reject the possibility. Wasn't it what I had most wanted for the last fifteen years? Did Ben really say, "It was always you, Julian"? I was certain I had heard just that. And yet the situation seemed bathed in unreality. I took my coffee with me to my desk to work for an hour or two. And then I showered and headed out to meet Ben.

He looked just as handsome in daylight as in the warm glow of restaurant lighting the night before. And Ben looked just as hot in jeans and a polo as he had looked when we were kids. We greeted each other. The host showed us to a table. We smiled. We ordered *café au lait* and some brunchy things. "Nice place," Ben said. "I thought Kayser was only in Paris."

"They're all over New York now," I said. "The pastries are pretty good. The bread, not so much, in my experience. But friends tell me they have some of the best bread in France. Who knows?"

"Jules, you look terrific—in case I didn't tell you that last night. I'm glad you've taken good care of yourself. I wish I could have been here to take care of you. But, well . . ."

"Ben, you're pushing my buttons. I don't know quite how to deal with you," I said.

"Everything used to be so easy with you—with us, Julian."

"Tell me," I said. "Those two years in that little studio apartment were the happiest of my life."

"If you don't want that again, then just tell me," Ben said. "But if you remember what we shared, and you want to try to get it back, then please don't waste this chance. I want it with all my heart. I was ambitious. I did what I believed I had to do. And I had some success—enough that Juilliard considers me a proper working professional who can teach from experience. I'm ready to land. All I want now is a good job and you. Will you have me?"

"Ben, this is crazy," I said. "Why would I trust you again? Why would I risk having you walk out on me again?"

"Julian, I'm not your mother," Ben said.

"No. I suspect she had bigger balls than you do." *Ouch!* I thought. *I didn't really say that, did I?* "Look, Ben, I'm sorry. I don't mean to be angry. I don't want to harbor resentment. It's just that if we look at history, we can see that you were supposed to be my lover—and I never confused you with my mother—and then one day you left me. It's pretty simple."

"You're right, Julian," Ben said. "I'm sure I don't deserve another chance at your love—another chance to build my life around yours. But I'm asking, just the same. Will you let me prove that I can get it right this time?"

"Come for the rest of the weekend, if you want to," I said. "We could give it a try. For the rest of today and tomorrow. No strings."

"You mean now? I don't have anything with me. All my stuff is back at the hotel."

"You don't need anything," I said. "I'm sure I can find an extra toothbrush, and I'll bet I can find something for you to wear, if you want to change. Think of it as a camping trip with a comfortable bed."

"Yes, Julian," Ben said. "I think that's a perfect idea. Leave it to you to come up with such a smart plan. Jules, there was never anyone but you."

"I think you should quit while you're ahead," I said. "I think you should come to my place and show me your heart—the one I don't know much about anymore. And then we'll see." And that's what we did.

Chapter Twenty

I liked welcoming Ben to my apartment. I had imagined having him there so many times through the years. He seemed to belong there, and yet? I began to regret my invitation. But then Ben kissed me, and all the years of anger and loneliness began to melt away. I was in Ben's arms, and nothing else mattered.

I led him to my bed, of course. We undressed and tumbled into it. I wasn't overthinking the situation. In fact, I stopped thinking at all and started feeling the warmth of Ben's embrace, the sweetness of his kisses, and the heat of his hands on my body. Was it as if we were twenty again? Nearly. The familiarity of Ben's body was comforting. He still had the same beautiful shoulders, the same handsome chest and sensitive nipples, the same flat stomach, and the same exquisite dick.

I reexplored all the well-loved territory. Every part of Ben was just as I remembered it, and yet just as exciting as the first time I discovered it. When I completed my tour, Ben started his. He visited every inch of me, from the top of my head to the tips of my toes. He caressed and nuzzled and tasted. When he had experienced the totality of my exterior, he kissed me deeply, yet again, and eased himself on top of me.

I accepted Ben's warmth and the reassuring pressure of his body on mine. We embraced as equals.

Ben waited patiently. I had forgotten—through the years—the thrill of total surrender to Ben's desire. It all came back to me in a rush of memory. I wrapped my legs around Ben's waist. I said, "Yes." And Ben took charge. He eased himself into position and gently arranged my legs on his shoulders. Ben leaned forward to kiss me as he presented his perfect dick. I accepted it. He slipped in as easily as if my interior had been his home always—as indeed it had been.

I began to cry a little, and so did Ben. The pleasure was even more exquisite than I remembered. We took our time. We shared a precious union. I wasn't certain where my body ended and Ben's began. It didn't seem to matter. We desired each other—totally. We trusted each other—totally. And when Ben was about to come, he kissed me and said, "Julian, I love you." And then he gifted me with his finest offering.

I was blissed-out, of course. It took me a while to come down from that high. Ben never released me from his embrace. "Julian, I don't know what to say."

"Then don't say anything," I suggested. "I could use a little nap," I said. "How about you?"

"As long as you'll let me hold you," Ben said.

"How could I refuse?" We did doze off for a bit. And when I woke Ben was still holding me. I gently disentangled our limbs. I was the one who got up first and headed to the john to pee. And on my way back to bed I got some robes for us. "What would you like for dinner?" I asked.

"Other than you?" Ben asked.

"Other than me," I answered.

"I don't care, Jules. I'll go out with you if you like, but I'd be just as happy to order something in. Why don't you decide for us?"

I ordered some things from the best pizzeria in the neighborhood. It was nearly like our student days, but with really sophisticated salad greens. I set the table. I opened a bottle of decent red. The delivery arrived. Ben and I sat at my table and shared a lovely supper. We both smiled a lot. Over coffee I asked, "Ben, how did the Juilliard thing happen, anyway?"

"I just found out who recommended me for the teaching post," Ben said. "I don't know his name, but there's a guy in the Met's costume department who's an old friend of the dean's. I think he's a wig-maker. I'm not sure how he knew about me, but he put in a good word." I was shocked, of course. It took me a few minutes to decide where to go with that new information.

"Ben, it's been a long day," I said. "I know I invited you for the weekend, but I'll have to do some work tomorrow if I'm going to meet my next deadline. Would you mind heading back to your hotel? Thanks for your visit. I'll call you—on Monday morning, if that's okay."

"Of course, Julian," Ben said. "I love you." He kissed me so sweetly that I was on the verge of a big Ben swoon. But I held firmly to my resolve.

"Go safely, Ben," I said. "I have a lot to think about."

"Yes, Julian. I understand." And he was gone. I felt in desperate need of a good night's sleep. I also felt in need of a good think. But my thoughts were racing so. Making sense didn't seem any more likely than sleep did. Michael helped Ben get to New York? How was that possible? I was in such a state that I was on the verge of losing my dinner. I sat quietly for a while. I poured myself a brandy. I sipped it. I decided to pull a Scarlett O'Hara and table the issue until morning.

I wouldn't call it sleeping, exactly, what I did that night.   I was like a pinball bouncing around a mattress factory. And then, finally, the sun came up. Hallelujah!

I phoned Michael first thing in the morning. "Could I see you? Soon?" I asked.

"I'm working today, but I should finish about 6:00. Will that work?"

"Of course," I said. "Why don't you come here, and we'll get some dinner?" I suggested.

"*Claro que sí.* I'll get there as early as I can. Thanks for your call, Julian. I've missed you."

"And I've missed you, too, Michael," I said. "More than you know." That was the truth, of course. And saying it out loud made me realize that I had missed Michael desperately in the last months. *How could I have ended our affair?* I wondered. *Michael's love is so solid. I could have counted on him. He could have been the anchor I always wanted. And now?*

I tried to put thoughts of Michael and Ben out of my head. It was a strange day, but I had plenty of work to do, so I forced myself to go to my desk and concentrate on the project at hand. It was another of those children's books I told you about. This one featured the topic of divorce, so it was a little disturbing. The sadness of dashed hopes and dreams always chills my blood. The author was so smart about teaching children they are not part of the failure. I tried to honor her vision. I worked. Evening finally arrived, as it always does.

Michael showed up promptly at 6:30. I embraced him warmly and sat him down at the counter while I poured a glass of wine. I said, "I thought maybe *tapas* tonight. There's a newish place on Second Avenue I hear good things about."

"Yes, so do I. Let's check it out." And that's what we did. The wait for a table was only about ten minutes. Michael and I mostly just looked at each other and smiled. Trying to have a conversation at a busy bar is always a challenge. We were seated, and we ordered some food. Little dishes began to arrive, full of color and deep flavors. Michael claimed they reminded him of a *tapería* in Madrid run by a family from Barcelona. And the fino sherry was excellent.

Over coffee and a shared order of *churros con chocolate,* I finally opened up: "Ben's in town. But then I think you know that."

"No, not really," Michael said. "But that's a good thing, yes?"

"I expect it's a very good thing for Ben," I said. "For me? I'm not so sure. Michael, please talk to me. What happened?"

"I only told my friend I know of a fine baritone who might be ready to settle down. The rest was up to them."

"Jesus, Michael!" I said. "How could you rear-range people's lives that way?"

"Julian, all I want is your happiness. If Ben makes you happy, then you should have him. If it were up to me, I'd want to be the one to try to make you happy for the rest of my life. But it isn't up to me. And so I did what I could. I don't think you understand how much I love you."

"I don't think I've understood much of anything, Michael," I said. "But I'm making some progress to-night. Will you come back to the apartment?"

"Of course," he said.

"Good. I have a little left in the bottle of Fundador you gave me. Perhaps you'll help me kill it."

Chapter Twenty-one

We headed back to my apartment. We sat at the counter. I poured. "Michael, I've made such a mess of things," I said. "I pined for Ben for fifteen years, and anything good that might have been possible I dismissed. Especially you. And now he's offered me what I wished so hard for. And I just don't want it. Michael, I don't want Ben. He's my past. He's a fine man. He'll make someone a wonderful husband. But not me." We sat quietly for a few minutes and sipped our brandy.

"It's good to know what we *don't* want," Michael said. "But what *do* you want?"

"I didn't have an answer to that question, maybe even yesterday. But I do now. Michael, I want *you. Te quiero, Miguelito. Te quiero muchisimo.* I hope I'm not too late. Will you have me?"

"On one condition," Michael said.

"Yes?"

"I'd like you to work on your Spanish. I want you to be comfortable when we go to Madrid in the spring."

"*Sí, señor.*" I lunged forward and grabbed Michael. He responded in kind.

"Will you marry me?" Michael asked.

"Yes," I said. "You don't even need to get on your knees, unless you want to, of course."

"Julian, you've made me the happiest man on Earth. We'll have a wonderful life together. I just know it."

"Yes, Michael. I know it, too." We adjourned to my bed to seal the deal with a kiss. Many kisses. We were both beaming with excitement, and contentment. "Do you really want me to meet your family?" I asked.

"Of course," Michael said. "Mother will adore you. She's a sucker for handsome men. Father will be gruff, but polite. He'll come around. I'm the youngest child, so he's always been a little more indulgent with me than with my brother and sister. And when he sees how happy you've made me, he'll love you almost as much as I do."

"I suppose we'll have to go to Connecticut, too. Dad has never known much of anything about my life. Perhaps it's time to change that."

"Maybe we should have the ceremony in April," Michael said. "Here? Or Connecticut? Or Madrid? We have choices these days."

"I love April," I said. "And could we marry in town? New York is our home. Let's start our new life together here. Chris and Becca will make beautiful groomsmaids."

"And maybe Stuart and Greg will stand up for us, too. And, I don't know if you knew this, but Van is licensed to perform ceremonies. I'm sure he'll want to officiate."

"Come here, you," I said. I embraced Michael as firmly as I dared.

Michael asked, "Julian, do you want to have children?"

"No, not really," I said, "but I'd be honored to bear your child if I could."

"Let's keep working on that."

"Michael, I think you'd be a wonderful father. I doubt I have it in me. But if it's what you want, then I'll take on a whole houseful of screaming brats. It's entirely up to you. Think about it. There's no reason to rush into a decision that important."

"You're right, Julian. There's no urgency there. But we do have to decide where we'll live," Michael said. "We're both so used to our spaces. You're more than welcome to move in with me. There's plenty of room, but then there's the matter of your office—and this wonderful bed. I'm sure *I'd* be very happy *here*, but I really don't want to give up my surroundings or my things."

"If we treat this as a professional apartment, then I think we can justify the expense of two rents. And the extra closet space would be a blessing. I think you'd probably find the kitchen easy to navigate—if we want to have a holiday party here, or something. And I wouldn't mind sleeping here now and then, just because. But I'll move in with you, Michael, if you'll have me."

"The sooner the better," he said.

"Michael, I'm exhausted. Could we get some sleep?" And that's what we did.

In the morning we had coffee and a bite. There were lots of smiles—and kisses. That time I gave Michael some of *my* clothes to wear, so he could get to work early in a fresh outfit. I loved the way he looked in the morning. I loved the way he filled out my jeans. I loved the way he loved me. I loved everything about him, really. I suppose I always had. And yet I hadn't really known it. Had I?

I went to my desk after Michael left my apartment. I was buzzing with excitement. There was work to do, as always. I got to it. I put off the call as long as I could, and then about 10:00 I phoned Ben. "Are you free at noon today?" I asked.

"Sure," Ben said. "Why don't you come to the hotel, and we'll find someplace to get a little lunch?"

"Perfect," I said. "I'll see you then."

That was done—or, rather, begun. And then I phoned Chris. That call was a welcome treat after the task that preceded it. She knew, of course, that Ben was in town. And she knew we had a Friday date. But I hadn't spoken to her since. "Dear, you're so smart about fashion," I said. "What should I wear to an April wedding?"

"It depends on the time of day, and—who's getting married?"

"Michael and me."

"Julian, you finally woke up! This is the best news I've heard in I-don't-know-when. Is Michael there?"

"No, he's working today," I said. "I'll see him tonight. Can I tell him you approve?"

"You can tell him I'm thrilled. Jules, this is wonderful. I want to give you two a party, or something. We'll figure it out. You've made me very happy, old friend."

"Not nearly as happy as Michael makes me. Chris, why do you suppose it took me so long to accept it?" I asked.

"Because you're stubborn. Because you're honest. Because you're loyal—sometimes, anyway. And maybe you were afraid of being abandoned again.

That's a very human fear—and a powerful one. What happened to change that?"

"Actually, I learned on Saturday night that Michael helped Ben get to New York. Michael just wants me to be happy. Anyway, I'll tell you about it soon, over dinner maybe," I said.

"Jules, stop analyzing it and just enjoy it."

"I intend to," I said. "But I still have to tell Ben."

"You'll find the words," Chris said. "And you'll see to it that Ben remains a lifelong friend." I wasn't so sure.

I was quite nervous. I tried to relax, and I tried to concentrate on staying on message. Ben was warm and welcoming, as always. He was charming. He was hot. Ben was the same man I fell so deeply in love with all those years before. And yet, everything else was different. We headed to a glorified coffee shop around the corner from his hotel. We ordered a glass of wine and a sandwich.

"Ben, I'm sorry I've kept you dangling since Saturday night," I said. "I had to think this all through carefully."

"Of course, Julian," he said. "This is about the rest of our lives."

"Ben, I can't do it. I can't try to pick up where we left off. I dreamed of us—together—for so many years. But—my heart moved on, I suppose. I have nothing but warm feelings for you. But no, I can't go back there."

"I'm sure I deserve that," Ben said. "I should never have left New York—and you."

"You did exactly what you needed to do at the time. And now you'll build a new life. Thank you for thinking I could be part of it. I have that on my record, anyway. Ben, you deserve to have everything easy and good in your life. I know you'll find it. Just not with me."

"Thank you, Julian, for considering my request. I hope we can be friends. We were always good friends, weren't we?"

"You have an excellent memory, Ben," I said. "We were the best of friends, as well as the best of lovers." *Shit!* I thought. *This is hard work. It hurts.* We were silent for a bit. We took some polite bites of our sandwiches, and then we asked the waitress to take them away. We ordered coffees. We toyed with them. I dreaded the next words that needed to be said.

"Ben, I have to be completely honest with you. You deserve that." He was silent. "I met someone— in the spring. Someone special. I sent him away, in early fall, because of the grip you've had on my heart all these years. And I just discovered that he's the man—the costumer at the Met—who put in a good word for you with the Dean of Vocal Studies at Juilliard.

"Ben, he hoped you'd come to New York. He was willing to exchange *his* happiness for *mine*. He loves me so much that he was prepared to help me build a life with another man. How could I not give Michael my heart? It was what I had wanted to do for months. But it didn't seem possible—until yesterday. Suddenly, my heart was my own—briefly, anyway. Until I gave it to Michael." There! I said it.

"Ouch!" Ben said. "That's a lot of information to process. I thought Juilliard wanted me for my talent and experience."

"Of course, Ben!" I said. "You know as well as I do that you were the perfect candidate for that job. Otherwise, you wouldn't have gotten the offer. It had nothing to do with me—or Michael. It's all about your credentials."

"I'll work on that concept," Ben said. "What are your plans?"

"Michael and I are getting married in April. Will you come to the wedding?"

"Only if you'll let me give you away."

"Oh, Ben. What a life we could have had together."

"If I had gotten things right," he said.

"I didn't say that."

"You didn't need to. I've been painfully aware of it for . . . never mind how long. Anyway, I want to meet Michael. Not this trip, I think. I really have to get back to Stuttgart. I'll finish up there and be in New York by Christmas. Perhaps we can all have dinner together during the holidays."

"Of course, Ben," I said. We rose to leave the coffee shop. Fall was always my favorite season in New York. The air feels crisp, and, yes, there is even the occasional scent of roasting chestnuts. Or perhaps that's just memory. Perhaps it's someone's fireplace instead. I put my arm in Ben's as we walked back to his hotel. We parted in front of it. We embraced warmly. "Have a safe trip," I said.

"Have a wonderful life," Ben said. I headed home in a fog of feelings. But I realized, as I got closer to the Upper East Side, that everything Ben—everything remembered and past—began to melt away.

Bruce K Beck

And everything Michael—everything real and pre-sent—began to surge through me like an electric current. I knew that I had chosen wisely, and that I would never second-guess my choice.

Chapter Twenty-two

The next weeks were busy ones. Moving in with Michael was a simple process. All I needed to bring to his apartment was a few outfits and warm jackets. And I bought duplicates of my favorite toiletries, so my apartment would stay functional. That's where I would be for at least part of most days, after all. That made the transition quite easy. I would have been willing to give up a lot to start a new life with Michael. But I was grateful that I didn't have to—give up the trappings of my old life.

The concert at Geffen Hall was glorious. Chris and Becca both were stellar. And the Philharmonic never sounded better. At one point, as the orchestra played the familiar introduction to *Voi che sapete*, who should walk on stage but a counter-tenor, rather than a mezzo. He was quite wonderful, and quite wonderful to look at, as well. I always felt uneasy with those breeches roles for mezzos anyway, although Rebecca was quite charming singing them. But I kidded her afterward, in the dressing room. I said, "Imagine that, Becca. A Cherubino with balls."

"I can imagine lots of things," she said. "For instance, I can imagine having yours on toast."

"With French butter, I hope," I said.

"I'll settle for Land o' Lakes," she said. "It's plenty good enough for homegrown meat."

"Remind me not to come to your kitchen, dear." I said.

"You can just stay in my heart, then. How's that, Little Julie?"

"Perfect," I said.

Chris's concerts at smaller venues were equally successful. It was a great month for her. She deserved it. Becca had a great month, too. She started dating a gorgeous guy she met at the gym. He was a personal trainer with the body of death and a very sweet nature. Rebecca had been without a steady for several years, so I was delighted for her.

As Thanksgiving approached, Michael and I had to decide how to celebrate. Neither of us had ever felt more grateful, so we wanted to get it right. Chris agreed to join us. Becca's boyfriend, Roy, was going to Virginia to be with his family, so she was willing to commit to our holiday feast as well. Van said yes. Stuart and Greg wouldn't be in town—Greg was in his fall semester and Stuart would be singing in Vienna—but they would be back in New York by Christmas.

"I don't know, *querido*," I said. "If we celebrate at home, then most of the cooking will fall to you, I'm afraid. I can maybe peel a sweet potato and trim a Brussels sprout, but roasting and gravy-making and all that jazz? As a cook, I make a good illustrator. I'm better off designing a graphic for the menu."

"I think we should go out this year," Michael said. "I think we should find a welcoming restaurant and just be really grateful that they're willing to feed our family."

"I think you're absolutely right," I said. "In fact, I think you're perfect. Have I told you that today?"

"Yes, but it's always nice to hear," Michael said. "Julian, I'm glad we'll be surrounded by friends on Thanksgiving, but I don't need anyone but you." I reached for Michael and wrapped my arms around him. That decision was made. What about the next decisions? It seems to be a season of choices. "Speaking of 'no one but you,'" Michael said, "I'm not willing to share you with anyone for our first Christmas together." I tightened my grip on the glorious man who wanted to bind his life to mine.

"I had a thought," I said.

"I quite like your thoughts, Julian. Especially when they have something to do with you and me and a big bed."

"This thought is a little different," I said. "This one is about New Year's Eve."

"And why can't that include you and me and a big bed?"

"It can," I said, "but I'm thinking we should go all out and get a table for the Met Gala."

"Perfect!" Michael said. "I can't think of a better way to usher in our new life together. I'll bet Chris and Van will join us, and Becca and Roy. I think Stuart and Greg will be in town."

"And Ben," I said. "We have to invite Ben."

"Of course we do," Michael said. "I'm glad you understand that. I'm glad you're not trying to erase Ben from your heart."

"It doesn't work that way, does it?"

"No," Michael said. "Fortunately. I know your love for me is not a replacement for your love for Ben. I get it. I'm just glad I have your love. I don't expect an exclusivity clause. I only expect a commitment. You've given me that. And I cherish it."

Bruce K Beck

"Come here, you!" I said. I had never really sensed anything like perfection in my life. But I certainly did then. And I could wrap my arms—and my heart—around it. "Please, Michael. Just hold me," I said. And he did. I was home. I was grounded. I was ready for whatever life had to offer.

The End

This is a first edition from
Audacity Books
Please visit us on the web at
www.audacitybooks.com
For information, please send your request to
info@audacitybooks.com.

OPERA OBSESSED is Volume 2 of Bruce K Beck's **Obsession Trilogy.** **INK OBSESSED** is Volume 1. Look for **THIS IS GOD'S COUNTRY**, Volume I of the **Tolerance Trilogy.** And the **Love Trilogy:** Volume I, **YOU'RE SURE TO FALL IN LOVE**, is set in Provincetown, MA, in the summer of 1976. **LOVE AND THE EPIDEMIC**, set in New York City in 1986, is Volume 2. Volume 3, **AND LOVE ENDURES**, is set in the early 1990s. For updates, and for occasional gifts and offers, please subscribe at:

www.audacitybooks.com/#subscribe

Many thanks to Sonya Teclai, Social Media Director at Audacity Books, for her support throughout the project. Particular thanks to Walter Maas for his generous wisdom. And to Richard Kutner for his classy edits. Tim Barber of Dissect Designs (www.dissectdesigns.com) signed on as a cover designer for my first novel, and he became a friend. You're Sure to Fall in Love, indeed. This journey would not have been possible without the example and the teaching of Joanna Penn at www.thecreativepenn.com. I am delighted, Joanna, to add this volume to your long list of books you have enabled. No doubt you will hit your one million mark any day now!

Bruce K Beck is both a writer and an accomplished chef. His novels, including the **Love Trilogy** and *THIS IS GOD'S COUNTRY* (**Volume I** of the **Tolerance Trilogy)**; are available online and wherever books are sold. Before turning to fiction, Beck authored *PRODUCE: A FRUIT AND VEGE-TABLE LOVERS' GUIDE*, which was called "gorgeous" by *The New York Times*, "a dazzler" by *Bon Appetit*, and "the most spectacular food book of the year" by *The Boston Globe*. His next book was *THE OFFICIAL FULTON FISH MARKET COOKBOOK*, which was called "invaluable" by Jacques Pépin, and "a treasure" by Irene Sax of *Newsday*. And Rex Reed said, ". . . you'll love this book. It's like a movie!"